War Bonds

BEVERLY JONES

Publication Manager – Gary Raham

Cover & Book Design – Tim Haley

On the cover: The author in her high school band uniform, 1945

ISBN-10: 0990482634
ISBN-13: 978-0-9904826-3-5

Penstemon
Publications

Penstemon Publications
Wellington, Colorado

"We have nothing to fear but fear itself."

~ FRANKLIN D. ROOSEVELT

Chapter 1

Uncle Sam Wants YOU!

C-*r-u-n-c-h!* Betsy back-peddled to brake – cringed at the spray of gravel – jumped off her bike and glanced at her watch.

"Hey, girlie! Don't you know there's a war on?"

She gritted her teeth. "Girlie." She *had* a name and he knew it. Besides, she sure didn't need him to point out that she'd just shaved off a layer of rubber from her already worn tires.

On top of it being so hot that heat waves rose from the sidewalk and her bike tires sank in the few streets that were paved plus being behind schedule, Harvey P. Slipher's "holier-than-thou" slur was the last thing she needed. A smart-aleck retort rode the tip of her tongue. But Mom's voice echoed in her ears... *Remember, Betsy, you're running a business. Always be courteous even when others are rude.*

She sucked in her breath and forced out words. "Good morning, Mr. Slipher." Busybody, she muttered to herself and hurried toward the post office door.

"Running late, are we?" His voice oozed sarcasm.

Betsy sensed him just behind her and pictured him with his thin black mustache, slimy with oil just like his hair. She decided not to answer. Then he was beside her.

"Well, if you want my advice," he warned, drawing out each word. Looking straight ahead, she said, "I won't be late." She squared her jaw, then remembering a new pimple had blossomed there this morning, slackened it.

Early this morning telephone wires had crackled with the news that a few prize scarcities like bananas and chocolate and maybe some sugar or meat would be delivered to the Mercantile. Mrs. Slipher would have been first to phone in her order.

Everyone said the Sliphers, who had only themselves and no children to feed, were hoarders. But Betsy also knew Mr. George, who ran the Mercantile grocery store, decided who got some of those scarce items and who didn't. He'd already called Betsy's mom to tell her he'd put some bananas and a pot roast aside for the Blakeslys. Betsy would stop in for her mother's groceries later.

Forget the Sliphers, Betsy told herself. In a few minutes she'd be walking into Mrs. Newton's red-and-white-checked kitchen filled with the spicy aromas of cookies just coming out of the oven.

The post office's lazy ceiling fan squeaked slow circles, but it might as well not be on for all the good it did. A handful of flies buzzed lazily, looking for a place to light, evading the sticky clutches of a long strip of flypaper. Straight ahead the big red, white, and blue poster announced in bold print: *"Uncle Sam Wants YOU!"*

That big, bony finger practically jumped from the poster at her, the piercing blue eyes framed by thick white brows and matching goatee underscoring the command. Well, he didn't really want her. She'd just turned fifteen, she wasn't a boy, and – even if she were – she wasn't old enough to register for the draft. Still, she was doing everything she could to help with the war fought from the home front. Everybody was, no matter what age. There were those few who didn't give it their all, but tried to make people think they were. Folks now and then whispered words like "draft dodgers," "hoarders," and buying things on the black market. People like this were a small minority.

"Mr. Mason!" Betsy called. She'd caught the postmaster just as he was ready to pull the mail pouch tight. "Mrs. Schlothauer's letter needs to go, please!"

"Ahh, just in the nick of time, Betsy." He smiled and took the thin V-mail envelope bordered with red and blue stripes. "In it goes! Be sure to tell her it's on the way to her son."

"You bet I will. Thanks, Mr. Mason!"

From the corner of her eye she saw Mr. Slipher deep in conversation with Mr. Van Brandt, president of the bank, and lost no time going back outside. She'd be here again soon with a load of packages to mail and by then a crowd of people would be shifting from one foot to the other near their boxes for the morning delivery. Maybe today she'd see a V-mail envelope slide into her family's box – news from one of Dad's three cousins overseas. Most of all she wanted to see Helen Martin's box stuffed with those V-mails. Helen had been waiting weeks to hear from her husband, Hal. He'd left before their baby son was born, so every day that passed without a letter worried Helen more.

Biking toward Oak Street, Betsy soon felt the shade of a cool canopy of thick-leafed elm, ash, and cottonwood trees lining both sides of the street. Only the songs of birds and voices of children – little girls playing with dolls under a willow tree, boys in a game of marbles – broke the quiet.

Dismounting at the front walk of the familiar brown frame house with its wide front porch, Betsy paused to breathe in the fragrance of Mrs. Newton's rose garden before walking her bike to the kitchen door. Just as she expected, tempting aromas of cinnamon and chocolate wafted through the screen. Her mouth watered, her stomach growled. At that moment Mrs. Newton swung open the door, cheeks rosy, fanning herself with her flour sack apron.

"Come in out of the heat, Betsy," she invited and motioned toward a white painted chair pulled out from the table. "Though I have to say it's almost as hot in here, what with the oven going all morning."

"Rest yourself, Betsy," Mrs. Sundstrom welcomed her. She was tall and large-boned with honey-colored hair like her two sons in the Navy, one on a submarine, the other assigned to an aircraft carrier. Betsy shivered. She couldn't imagine being deep beneath the surface of the ocean, wondering if enemy ships were near or being torpedoed by the enemy. And aircraft carriers – like the one her aunt's husband was assigned to – were so out in the open, sitting targets it seemed.

But now, with a satisfied sigh, she sank onto the offered chair.

Mrs. Taylor, the smallest of the three ladies, slid a plate of not-quite-perfect cookies across the table, then took a pitcher of lemonade from the refrigerator.

"Maybe we'll rest ourselves a moment, too," she said. "I declare I don't remember a hotter summer than this and today sure 'takes the cake." She took off her wire-framed glasses, wiped perspiration from her face with her handkerchief, and announced, "One more box to wrap and a handful more to label."

Mrs. Newton's shoulders sagged as she surveyed the clutter of batter-spattered pots and bowls, measuring cups and mixing spoons, broken eggshells, and cookie sheets stacked helter-skelter on the kitchen counter and in the sink. "Those," she proclaimed, joining the others at the table, "can wait."

With a fan blowing, the room truly did feel cooler. Betsy was hungry enough to devour whatever they put in front of her. Manners, she reminded herself, and reached for a spice cookie, secretly grateful for the ones deemed imperfect to pack by the ladies. After all – she reasoned – a person serving on the home front had to have an energy boost, too, didn't she?

"Ummm…this cookie's really swell, Mrs. Newton." Drinking deep from the tall cold glass, she patted her lips with the red-and-white checked cotton napkin. "And the lemonade hits the spot. I'm so thirsty!"

"We used all the sugar for baking, Betsy," Mrs. Sundstrom said, "or we could have sweetened it with sugar instead of honey." She urged the cookie plate toward Betsy.

"I like tart lemonade better than sweet. Honest. And the cookies – ummm! out of this world." The final bitter traces of her encounter with Mr. Slipher dissolved along with the last bite of a brownie on her tongue.

She stood and carried her empty glass to the sink. "May I help with these last few packages?"

"That you could," Mrs. Newton said, holding a nearly used up ball of heavy string – string made up of varying lengths and sizes tied together to make one whole. No one threw away a piece of string, no matter how short. "I need a strong thumb to hold the knot when I'm ready to tie it."

Betsy saw that besides the separate packages of cookies, the box also held reminders of home like a *Reader's Digest*, this week's issue of the *Plainview Sun*, Pepsodent tooth paste, Lifebuoy soap, all three flavors of Wrigley's gum, a pair of hand-knit socks to be worn in most any kind of weather, but especially when winter came. Of course the ladies who boxed packages and rolled bandages for the Red Cross sent many of these items and more, but it was this team of three who baked and boxed homemade goodies. All the housewives in town contributed ingredients scrimped from their families' food rationing books. Everyone knew that mail call boosted the troops' morale when they were so far from home. Being a part of it boosted Betsy's morale, too.

Mrs. Taylor began counting the boxes, each wrapped with heavy brown paper, tightly bound with string, and labeled with names of Plainsview boys in the military – and two girls, one a Red Cross nurse, the other in the Waves. "Six more this time," she said, sighing. "If the war doesn't end soon...." her voice drifted off.

Mrs. Sundstrom hurried to fill the silence. "Yes, and I'm afraid you'll need to make more than one trip to the post office again, Betsy," she said, shaking her head. "We'd sure be in a pickle without Betsy's Wartime Delivery Service!"

"All those stores – even the ones in Denver – that used to deliver goods right to our doors without charge spoiled us," Mrs. Taylor said. "I wonder if delivery trucks will ever come back even after the war's over."

"No use thinking about that now." Mrs. Sundstrom set her pen and bottle of ink aside, then added the last package to the stack.

Just then the phone rang, "Who could that be?" Mrs. Newton raised her eyebrows. "Everyone knows this is our 'goodies from home' package morning and wouldn't disturb us if it weren't...." Her forehead wrinkled in a worried frown.

"Hello," she said into the mouthpiece on the wall, holding the receiver to her ear, "this is the Newton residence." When she heard the voice at the other end of the line, the frown of worry changed to a frown of vexation.

"Yes, Mrs. Slipher, Betsy's just leaving here for the post office." Mrs. Newton looked across the room at Betsy. Betsy heard the other two ladies murmur something to each other. "Yes, I'll tell her. And don't fret. She'll have your grocery order at your kitchen door with time to spare before lunch. But the servicemen's packages come first, I'm sure you'll agree."

Betsy stifled a groan as Mrs. Newton replaced the receiver on the hook and walked back into the kitchen. "Mrs. Slipher wants you to take the groceries in without knocking and set them on the kitchen table," she directed Betsy. "She can't be disturbed during today's episode of 'The Romance of Helen Trent.' Don't wait to be paid. She doesn't have any dimes."

Mrs. Sundstrom rolled her eyes. Mrs. Taylor clicked her tongue, "How many dimes does she already owe you?"

All three began carrying packages out to Betsy's bike. Even with her oversized handlebar basket, the wooden orange crate fastened to the rear fender, and her brother Bobby's red wagon tied to the back, she'd have to make a second trip. Betsy rolled her jeans up another notch. Couldn't risk getting a pant leg caught in the chain.

"Hey, there, Snub Nose!" Jack Gordon whizzed up on his bike, nodded at the ladies. "I see you home bakers are at it again – those lucky guys!"

Jack Gordon. Betsy felt her face flush. Why wasn't he at the bakery working?

"Mighty big load you've got, Miss Betsy B.! Here, I'll lend a hand. Is this it or are there more?"

She put one foot on a pedal and gave him the look. "I can manage."

But Mrs. Taylor was on her way back to the kitchen. "What a help that would be, Jack. Come in and finish off the last of the cookies and a glass of milk while I collect the rest of the boxes."

Mrs. Sundstrom checked to make sure nothing would topple off. Mrs. Newton slid an envelope of money into the bag tied around Betsy's waist, saying, "This should cover the mailing cost for all the packages, dear. The Ladies Aid sure does a fine job of rounding up money for postage. And I've added in your delivery fee. More savings stamps toward your War Bond!"

Another bond drive was coming up soon. *"Bonds for Bombs"* was the slogan. For Betsy, buying a bond when she could was another part of the war effort with the bonus that later she could use her bonds to help pay her way to college. She knew Dad's salary couldn't support the family and send her to college, too, though he – along with Mom – was determined that somehow Betsy would graduate from college, just as both of them had.

"Thanks, all of you," Betsy said. "I'll go on ahead. Jack's sure to catch up with me." What a showoff! He'd whiz past and beat her to the post office door.

She'd barely gotten herself balanced on the bike when there he was.

"Hey, your load's way too heavy." He skimmed packages from the top of each bundle and tucked them securely under one arm. The ones he'd taken from the kitchen were already clutched in the other. And off he rode – no hands on the handlebars – whistling the Air Force tune, "Off we go – into the wild blue yonder...." Betsy knew the minute Jack turned 18, he'd be off to serve in that branch of the military – if they gave him a choice. Like some of the other boys just under draft age, Jack probably believed that *"Uncle Sam Wants You"* poster meant *him.*

CHAPTER 2

He's Watching YOU!

T he bag of morning mail had just arrived when Betsy and Jack pushed into the post office, staggering under their load of packages. Postmaster Mason looked up from sorting and motioned toward the weighing scale. "One for my boy in there?" he asked, one silver-flecked eyebrow lifting in a question.

Betsy nodded. "Saw it with my own eyes!"

Together, Betsy and Jack lined up the securely wrapped bundles, then walked to the wall of mailboxes to join other townspeople already waiting – the young, the old, women *(most past their 20s)* – everyone eager for a letter from loved ones near or far, the latest edition of *Life* magazine with its extra size pages of war scene photos, *The Saturday Evening Post* – sure to arrive with the latest homey cover painted by Norman Rockwell, *Time*, which her parents read from cover to cover, *Reader's Digest* –small and easy to flip through and choose which section to read (she liked the vocabulary tests and humor pieces best). And *Calling All Girls*, Betsy's very own magazine with articles and fashions meant for girls like her.

She shook away her daydreaming. The air in the room felt heavy. Heavy with something more than record mid-summer heat. Something that had the feel of a nervous undertone – people talking low among themselves even as they glanced with hope in their eyes at the windows of their mailboxes. Betsy caught snatches of the talk.

"...trainload of 'em comin' in..." one man with a gravelly voice said.

"But the camp's not finished. Where...?" a woman protested.

"Tents," came the curt answer. "Rows of 'em."

Tents? Were they talking about the war prisoners? Betsy shivered.

"Shoulda run that Sam Albertson outta town last spring when he sold us out to the gov'ment." The words ended with a snarl.

Betsy thought back a few months to how people grumbled when the government chose a section of Mr. Albertson's prime farmland. Instead of this year's crops the prisoner of war camp would soon rise on that plot of earth. She hadn't paid much attention then, but now – well, as the whole community watched the camp rise on that hill outside of town, it sure seemed close.

Someone else said, "Blame FDR, that's who. Dad-gum Democrat."

Betsy's heart skipped a beat. She looked up at Jack.

A year older than Betsy, Jack didn't come close to resembling everyone's image of the "All American boy" – he had a nose like that of an eagle, a body so skinny kids called him "Slats." But the thing that really got on her nerves was that unbearably cocky grin. Still, he was tall. There wasn't a fellow in her sophomore class taller than she was, and it made her feel better somehow to look up at a boy instead of trying to shrink down.

But all this post office talk – Jack gave her a sharp look. "You guessed it," he said. "Trainload of prisoners of war headed our way. But, hey, not something to worry about. They'll be locked inside that camp. American soldiers standing guard."

Even so, she thought, what if...?

Sensing her doubt, he said, "Look at it this way, Betsy B. – here we are on the home front and just got handed a piece of the war front. Enemy soldiers captured in battle. That many fewer Nazis on the battlefield against our troops."

To see it his way, she'd have to shift her mental gears into – what? Not "reverse," but she couldn't name a gear that would steer her that direction. Sure, they'd had plenty of advance notice. Everyone had marveled at the high barbed wire fence, barracks and watchtowers, searchlights, snarling dogs. Why, they'd even planted some long rows of trees. The news articles and editorials in the weekly issues of the *Sun* reporting the progress of the camp, assuring readers they were safe and reminding readers that farmers needed the prisoners to work in the fields. And always warning readers not to "fraternize with prisoners."

Still she couldn't help feeling an edge of fear. A collage of images – black and white newsreels showing Nazi soldiers goose stepping, vivid photos in *Life* magazines, banner headlines, countless war posters swirled through her imagination. Most ominous of all – that dark poster she avoided looking at, the one labeled: "He's watching you," the he *(a Nazi?)* whose only features, a shrouded pair of steely eyes, showed through the medieval looking armor, helmet pulled close, bayonet erect. Despite the shimmering heat, she shivered, then told herself to focus on other posters – ones for war bond drives, scrap drives, American Red Cross nurses pert and capable wearing starched white dresses and skirts with blue capes and airplane pilots with metal wings on their jackets and keen eyes looking skyward, the bright letter "V" for Victory against a white background.

In spite of reading the news and riding along that road and seeing the camp grow, it hadn't seemed real. Till now. Suddenly it was like the enemy had landed in her own back yard.

But something more was clouding the air in the post office – something in the tone of the talk. An undertow tugging beneath the surface of the words. Another thing, why did that man bring up being a Democrat loud enough for Mr. Mason to hear? Of course Mr. Mason was a Democrat: law required that the postmaster be a member of the same political party as the President. Yet in Plainsview it seemed most grownups were Republicans and thought Democrats were almost as bad as Catholics. Or Jews. What did belonging to a particular party matter? Betsy couldn't make sense of that. Mr. Mason worked hard and had a smile and friendly greeting for everyone. He and his family were "doing their part" for the war effort lots more than some families. The Masons' son, Eddie, was training to serve on a Navy submarine, their older daughter, Midge, worked the night shift in a California war weapons factory that manufactured battle ships. Emily, the youngest, was one of Betsy's best friends and an honor student. Republicans, Democrats. Wasn't being an American the main thing?

Just then Betsy saw – one, no, maybe three or more – V-mails appear in the window of Helen Martin's box. She forgot everything but grabbing those thin as onion peel envelopes and delivering them into Helen's hands. Standing on tiptoe, she twirled the combination – two to the right, three to the left, then one more to the right. The little door swung open, she reached in and pulled out the bundle of V-mails looking battle-weary, each addressed in Hal Martin's strong, sprawling handwriting. Writing Betsy recognized at once.

Jack grinned, the ever-present mischief sparking from his clear blue eyes. "Go, goof-ball," he said. You can be back in plenty of time to pay the shipping costs."

He stepped aside to let her pass.

"Tell Mr. Mason I'll be back in a few minutes." Betsy swept past, then glanced over her shoulder. "Oh, and – thanks, Jack."

He swept a bow. "Glad to be of service, Miss Blakesly. Me, I've got to hustle back to the bakery soon as I collect our mail and make sure the ladies' boxes are ready to go!"

Betsy sped off toward the Martins' home. Helen, an apron over her forget-me-not cotton print housedress, stood watching on the front porch, little Ginny humming to herself in her green wicker rocking chair. Baby Tommy slept on his mother's shoulder. The moment Helen saw Betsy waving the letters, her face lit up.

"These just came in, Helen," Betsy announced, fanning them out. "A bundle of them!"

"Mommy! Mommy! Read them out loud!" Ginny, her light brown Shirley Temple curls bouncing, danced to her mother's side, looked up and said politely, "Pretty please with sugar on it."

"Oh, Betsy, thank you!" Helen blinked away the tears brimming in her eyes. "It's been – well, it's been *forever* since we've heard from him, and...."

"You're welcome, Helen. I'm so happy these were in your box."

She paused a moment before leaving, wanting to linger a little longer in the circle of the little family's glow.

She watched Helen settle herself and the two children on the porch swing – Ginny nestled close, brown-eyed Tommy on her lap – and begin turning the envelopes over and over, holding them, making this moment last before opening them. The letters meant Hal was still alive, still safe, at least he was when he wrote them.

Feeling warm inside, Betsy turned and pedaled away, mentally checking off her list – post office first, then Mrs. Slipher's grocery order. Ugh. The radio would be blasting today's fifteen-minute segment of *"The Romance of Helen Trent,"* the spoiled yippy nippy lap dog, Phoophie, clicking her toenails on the kitchen linoleum. After that she could escape for lunch at home. Her stomach was growling and she was bursting to tell Mom about her morning. That is if Miss big ears, big mouth sister Cat could sit still a few minutes and Billie was in his own world playing aviator with his squadron of toy airplanes.

She parked her bike outside the post office and went in to pay Mr. Mason, then collect the mail from the Blakeslys' box. Adjusting her eyes to the light inside the building, she found herself staring right at that sinister black poster printed with the warning: *"He's watching YOU."*

She turned away, tucked the mail in her pouch, and walked out into the noon heat. As she rounded the corner to head for the Sliphers' home, a dog's howls drew her up short. A half dozen or so boys – not quite old enough for junior high – were throwing rocks, kicking, and grabbing a dog so thin his ribs showed. The mutt bared his teeth and tried to twist away but couldn't.

"Beat it, Kraut!" one boy yelled, kicking the dog's back haunch.

"No good bag of bones." Another boy picked up a rock in the street, aimed it, and made a direct hit. The dog yelped, turned, and limped off, scraggly tail between his legs.

Betsy grabbed the ringleader by the arm. "You big bully. Pick on somebody your own size. And leave your buddies behind."

The kid wrenched away from her, caught up with the dog, too crippled to have gone far, and kicked him again. "Dumb dog's trespassin'. Belongs across the tracks with all the other dirty Krauts." He glared at Betsy.

Betsy stared him down. Freckles peppered across his nose, his ears stuck out, and his hair spiked like out-of-control carrot sprouts. The red hair gave him away – Colleen Sherman's kid brother. Colleen's hair was red, too, only hers was auburn, the envy of every girl at school and sent the boys trailing after her. If those little hoodlums weren't painting the Taylors' cat green, they were waiting for a chance to pick on the Rainsfords' retarded boy.

Betsy clenched her teeth. "You're Colleen Sherman's brother, Spud, aren't you."

"For me to know and you to find out." He sniffed, feet planted wide apart, hands on his hips. "Besides, ain't none of your bees wax."

Betsy turned up her nose and pushed off.

Spud's taunt followed her, "See ya' around, *sugar tramp.*"

Betsy's temper flared. Sure, her dad – like other men at Great Western Sugar – called themselves "sugar tramps," not because they were tramps like hobos, catching rides on box cars and knocking on doors to beg for food, but because the company required the family to move – "tramp" – to a different sugar plant town when a promotion was offered. Company people used the term without even thinking, but the way Spud said it made her feel like a scumbag.

She pedaled as fast as her legs would go, letting her temper cool. Eyes straight ahead, she passed the row of dark windows of the billiards parlor, cigarette and cigar smoke billowing from the door that sat ajar. She pedaled even faster to do her next errand.

CHAPTER 3

Kilroy Was Here

A cheery voice called from across the street. "Hello there, Betsy. You're looking kinda downhearted. What's going on?"

Betsy crossed over to where Fred Hopper stood on a ladder painting the latest names on the Honor Roll board – names of Plainsview young people serving in the military. Two years' worth of them and the list growing longer every week. She remembered how on Pearl Harbor Day men had bragged that the Americans would win the war in a few weeks. They weren't bragging now. The Honor Roll Board was proof. As the fighting grew worse, the draft board had begun calling up boys who were 18 but hadn't yet graduated from high school, along with men in their late 20s and early 30s. Square white banners bordered in red and centered with a blue star – sometimes two or three – now showed up in living room windows up and down each block. A star for each family member serving in the military. Then gold stars began to replace some of the blue ones. Gold for a son or husband who'd lost his life.

Fred was of draft age, but his card said "4-F." He might be crippled, but he did more than his share on the home front. And the way he painted those names seemed to give them a sense of the sacred. Each letter sharp and clear. No smears or drips. She watched as he formed the final "r" on "Henry C. Schott, Jr." Her chest tightened. Hank, drafted the day he graduated, had played tuba in the high school band and, oh, how he loved playing ooom-pahs over and over and with many variations. Having fun, making the rest of the band members laugh. Now. . . .

Fred wiped his brush on a rag, said, "So, Miss Betsy, what's troubling you? Out with it."

She took a deep breath, spilled out the story of Spud Sherman and his gang's latest mean trick.

The smell of turpentine was strong as Fred cleaned his brush, then took a step down from the ladder. He pulled off his cap, wiped perspiration from his face, shook his head. "What those boys need is a trip to the proverbial wood shed involving an extra big strop. Followed by not being allowed to leave the house for a month except for doing a list of supervised good deeds."

Betsy grinned. "I doubt that Spencer Sherman has ever gotten much harsher punishment than a frown or a three-word scolding."

She settled onto her bike seat. "I'd better get on with my errands, Fred. Thanks for hearing me out!"

"Hey, what are friends for?" Fred turned and dipped his brush into the pot of blue paint.

At lunch, Mom listened quietly to Betsy's recitation of her roller coaster morning. Billie, who'd soon be five, clutched a toy fighter plane and leaned into the table. Mom handed him a napkin to wipe the peanut butter and grape jam off his face. "Those boys are naughty," he said, punctuating the sentence with a frown.

Cat – alias Miss Nosy, age 10 – balled up her fist. "I bet I could beat up on all of them. What a bunch of chickens."

"They'll get what's coming to them one of these days," Mom predicted, giving Cat a hard look. "And, all three of you, I don't want you worrying about the war prisoners moving into camp. I know it feels strange to have them right here, but strange things happen in war." She swept a stray lock of hair from her forehead, a few silver ones flecking the brunette. "Remember, they're in a secure army prison camp. We'll talk about it more at supper when Dad's here." It was understood that before any talk could begin, they'd be listening to Edward R. Murrow's six o'clock news broadcast.

Betsy helped clear the dishes from the table and stack them in the sink. Cat put the milk bottle and a big red apple in the refrigerator.

Energized, Betsy was ready for this afternoon's errands even if it was still hot. The hard part of the day was done. Just one afternoon delivery and then she'd promised to walk Mom's friend's new baby in his buggy for an hour.

"'Bye, Mom. See ya, Cat – Billie," she called and stepped out the back door to grab her bike.

But her bike was gone. A chalk figure stared up at her from the sidewalk:

CHAPTER 4

Rescue Mission

C at was out the door, Mom and Billie close behind. Staring at the Kilroy cartoon, Cat sputtered, "Kilroy, my eye! That's Spud and his gang." She looked at Betsy. "Getting even with you, I bet!"

Mom shook her head, shaded her eyes and scanned the back yard.

Betsy moaned, "M-o-o-o-m, what am I going to do? I need my bike! I'll be late doing Mrs. Keller's errand."

Mom took charge. "Good thing you untied Billie's wagon before lunch. Take it now and get the errand done. The three of us will look around the neighborhood. They can't have gone far with it."

"Billie?" Betsy asked.

Billie, fastening his black aviator hat under his chin, didn't even hesitate. "Sure, Betsy. Take it."

Betsy nodded, grabbed the wagon handle, called, "I'll be back as soon as I can – with my bike if you don't find it first."

Cat had her own plan. "Hey, I'll find Spud and make him tell!"

Mom frowned. "No, Carol. That would make things worse. You stay with Billie and me."

Cat knew Mom meant it when she said "Carol" in that tone. "Well, if you say so, Mom, but – " she grumbled. "And after we find the bike, I'm going to rescue that poor dog."

Mom untied her apron strings and sighed. "Oh, no, not another needy animal in the house."

How many creatures had Cat rescued? Or tried to? Betsy wondered, listing those she remembered. There'd been that sparrow with a broken wing, a nest of abandoned robin's eggs, a water snake – not to rescue but just for fun – a mangy, hissing black cat. And the field mouse. Mom had let out a shriek on that one and sent Cat out, cradling the mouse, its skinny-tail twitching.

The search team headed out into the neighborhood. Betsy turned toward Main Street, red wagon in tow. A mix of anger and humiliation churned inside her. Well, no sense whining. She couldn't let her customers down.

Three stops for Mrs. Keller's order – Pete's Drugs, the Mercantile, and Bernie's Bakery. Mrs. Keller *would* want something at the bakery. Jack was sure to be at the counter ready to tease her as usual about did she mean this or did she mean that, making her cheeks flush in embarrassment. Today was definitely not her lucky day.

Betsy pulled the wagon through alleys, looked inside trash bins, peered into every doorway and dark corner, opened the door of an empty shed, and threaded through a row of thick bushes as she trudged from the drugstore to the Mercantile, and on to the bakery. No bike. She didn't know whether to scream or to cry. She tried to hide her frustration as she stepped inside the bakery, the bell on the door announcing her presence.

Sure enough, out from the kitchen came Jack, looking skinnier than ever in that tall, goofy white baker's hat, a flour- and dough-spattered apron tied at his waist.

"Well, Miss Betsy B.," he said, "what'll it be today?"

"Mrs. Keller's order," she blurted. "Oh, and for my mother a loaf of bread and a dozen raised doughnuts."

"White or wheat, glazed or sugared?"

He said it so fast Betsy had to ask him to say it again. She stammered, "Ummmm – *white* bread, *glazed* doughnuts."

"Coming right up!" he said and snapped open two white paper bags. He handed her Mrs. Keller's order, then rang up the bill on the cash register: bread a dime, a baker's dozen doughnuts a quarter. Betsy dug into her coin pouch.

Handing her the baked goods, Jack glanced out the store window. "So what are you doing with your little brother's wagon? I thought you and your bike were practically glued together."

Without warning, tears welled her eyes. It was hard to blink them back.

"Hey," Jack said, the teasing in his voice gone, "I'm sorry, Betsy, I didn't mean. . . ."

"It's not you, Jack, it's. . . ." The story of Spud and his gang tumbled out for the third time. "And now Mom and Cat and Billie are searching the neighborhood and I've looked everywhere I could while I was running Mrs. Keller's errand and I saw both Fran and Mary Beth, and asked them to be on the lookout."

Jack's thick eyebrows met in a frown. "Sounds like one of Spud's nasty tricks, all right."

He pulled out a man's handkerchief and handed it across the counter.

"Hey, Betsy, I'll see if I can get off work early, jump on my bike, and give you a lift. We'll find that bike of yours, and that's a promise – okay?"

Oh swell, Betsy thought, her stomach turning over. He was going to put her on the handlebars of that tall, skinny bike and ride off like a tornado. Well, she wasn't going to let him know she was scared out of her wits just thinking of it.

After her hour of pushing the sleeping baby in his buggy, all the time keeping her eyes out, there wasn't a sign of her red bike. All the girls she knew had blue bikes with the new style balloon tires – Dad had asked a friend he knew to put hers together with parts he found. It had come back looking brand new – the frame was bright red, shiny metal fenders fit the narrow tires Dad said could go faster than the balloon type, and the handlebars, too, were more slender and easier to steer than other bikes. She'd know it anywhere.

Clearly Mom's search trio hadn't found it either or Cat would be running to meet her. Instead, Cat looked at Betsy and shrugged her shoulders. "We searched this neighborhood inside out before Mom put Billie down for a nap. You could tell how mad she was when she started banging pots and pans around in the kitchen."

"We can't let those smart alecks outsmart us, Cat. Jack's going to help after he gets off work. Maybe it takes a teenage fellow's brain to figure out what might be going on in a kid like Spud Sherman's head."

Betsy went into the bathroom and splashed cold water on her face. That's when she heard Jack's familiar whistle and a knock on the back screen door.

"Think you should report this to the cop – whatshisface?" Cat asked.

"Last thing I'd do. First of all, he's blind as a bat, slower than molasses, and even if he did find the bike and go after Spud, you can bet Spud and his gang would spend years getting revenge." Betsy shook her head and told Mom where she was going.

"Jack'll find the bike, Betsy. He's no moron," Cat said. "Me – I'm going to rescue that poor mutt."

When Jack rode up, he patted the handlebars. "Passenger seat... guaranteed to get you to your destination safe and sound."

She hoped he couldn't hear her heart thudding like a bass drum. Suddenly his bike was higher and narrower than she'd thought! This was sure going to be a scarier ride than the Wild Cat at Denver's Lakeside Amusement Park. Somehow she got herself up and more or less seated, her hands glued to the metal handlebars in a white-knuckled grip.

Jack zipped along side streets, winding in and out of places she'd never have thought of. All at once he headed for the Conoco gas station. "I've got a hunch. Let's conduct a little investigation."

At the back of the building he slowed, then braked, held the bike steady while Betsy got off, let out her breath, glad to plant both feet on firm ground. What was he thinking? She'd never looked behind a filling station before, but Jack was peering down into some sort of dark cavern.

"Grease pit," he said. "Where they grease cars and trucks. I'm going to let myself down."

Betsy looked around, wondering if Wayne, the manager, was in the station.

Just then Jack shouted, "Found it!"

Betsy's heart skipped a beat.

"I'm going to heave it up. Be ready to grab hold of it, okay?"

The bike appeared at the edge of the cement pit, Betsy grasping and tugging, then finally easing it onto the ground. Her breath caught. "Oh, Jack, look!"

The bike was hers, all right, but barely recognizable. How could anyone – even Spud Sherman – do this to her bike? And it was hers, all right – fire engine red and shiny aluminum.

Now, like rewinding newsreels before the main feature at the movies, memories of those days before the war played across the screen of her mind's eye. One of her favorites from the town they'd lived in before Plainsview – just after getting her bike on her 12th birthday riding with a couple of friends on a summer day along country roads, gravelly and rutted, to see their classmate Phyllis on the Petersons' farm. Hens, roosters, and chickens scratching for table scraps and kernels of dry corn, barn cats frisking through the loft, all four girls sliding down the straw stack, shrieking – sharp stubs prickling inside their shirts – Phyllis's father, two older brothers along with the hired hand repairing farm machinery, then steering the John Deere tractor up and down rows of rich earth. A monster-size tire swing hanging from a thick rope on the stout branch of the cotton-wood tree where it was always shady and cool.

Mrs. Peterson laid extra plates on the table for lunch when the girls rode their bikes out. She'd set a dishpanful of warm water, a bar of Lifebuoy soap, and a towel on the back porch and tell the girls to wash first before the sweaty, sunburned men with dirt and grease under their fingernails had their turn.

Hungry as she was by noon, she secretly hoped dinner would be fried chicken – or "sshick'n" as Phyllis's mom pronounced it – and not cod – the Petersons' favorite from the old country. The mere smell of it made Betsy gag. She tried her best to be polite and take a few bites. But when it was fried chicken – two or three butchered and cleaned by Mrs. Peterson that morning before pan-frying the pieces – bowls with mashed potatoes and gravy, home-churned butter melting over string beans and plates of sliced red tomatoes and cool cucumbers from the garden, bread straight from the oven, a tall glass of cold milk from the Petersons' cows – Betsy found it hard to mind her manners and wait while the serving bowls passed from hand to hand around the table and Mr. Peterson took the first bite, signaling everyone could eat now. Betsy watched wide-eyed at how the men helped themselves to second and third helpings of everything.

After a day on the farm, Betsy and her friends pedaled at a snail's pace back to town, bodies grimy and itchy, sweaty and bone-tired. And yet – and yet – lifted with a sense of pure contentment.

~

Betsy thought back to those pre-war days when the bike was for pleasure or getting from one place to the next. Sunday, December 7, 1941 turned that world upside down. Her grandparents had driven from Denver for dinner – Mom's tender pot roast with homemade noodles and bowls of chocolate ice cream Dad had brought home from Jud's ice cream parlor – a warm December day marked by the usual Sunday afternoon slowness of time, the kind of day that beckoned Betsy, restless with grownup talk, outdoors to ride her bike up and down the street. Suddenly her ears perked up to the sound of Dad's familiar, thin three-note whistle.

Were Grandma and Grandpa leaving already? She stepped inside, saw the family huddled in front of the polished walnut RCA radio console, an eerie hush filled the room.

President Roosevelt spoke in somber tones. The Japanese, he announced, had attacked Pearl Harbor. That moment – those words – were stamped on Betsy's memory forever – Dad's jaw tightened, his forehead furrowed; Mom's smile vanished, her face blank with shock; Grandpa took Grandma's hand in his – sounds drifted in from outside – their neighbors talking across fences, some in low tones, others loud and indignant.

War was declared and the nation focused on the war effort. Because of rubber and gas shortages, stores no longer made home deliveries. That's when Betsy came up with the idea of Betsy's War Time Delivery Service. She put an ad in the paper and soon the phone began to ring. Adding an orange crate to her back fender to supplement the bike basket, she rode off on her first day of service. That was two years ago.

And her delivery service was needed more every day. Now

the only wartime mission her bike seemed good for was the next scrap drive.

She felt Jack's hand on her shoulder. "Betsy," he said, "I know it looks bad, but it can be fixed. Let me take it home. Dad's got a shop filled with tools. I'll get some help and we'll get your bike back in action. For the war effort."

CHAPTER 5

Freedom from Fear

"Phew – ee! I'm going outdoors." Billie pinched his nostrils together and skipped out the back door, muttering something about "girl stuff."

It was Sunday afternoon and one end of the kitchen table was spread with Toni Home Permanent paraphernalia – printed directions, a couple of old bath towels, comb, curlers, and bowls of bad-smelling chemicals. Though it was not their favorite thing to do, both Mom and Betsy were glad an inexpensive home perm had been invented. Up to now the only way to get a perm had been at the beauty parlor where the price was too high for most people's budgets, required tedious hours of moving from one station to another and ending up sitting hooked inside a metal helmet over a head peppered with rollers attached to individual wires. And for Betsy it would mean walking out the door with frizzy hair. Mom hadn't learned how to be a beautician, but she followed the kit's directions and learned the right time to rinse out each of the chemicals so Betsy's curls would result in soft waves easy to shampoo, set in curlers, then brush and comb. Mom made their own war time shampoo by saving bar soap chips and melting them in an enameled pot... after a vigorous scrubbing, she rinsed the clean hair first in tap water, then poured a glass of vinegar mixed with warm water to keep the tangles away and give a shine to her hair.

Perms at home took only a couple of hours. Here, they could relax and talk. Like this afternoon when Betsy's friends Fran and Mary Beth, seated at the other end of the table, had arranged an assembly line with the makings of jewelry – dried chicken wishbones, macaroni shells, two shades of nail polish, and bowls of water colored with red, yellow, and blue food dye. Plus plenty of string, yarn, and a pair of scissors. They'd gotten the idea from the latest issue of *Calling All Girls*. Now they'd each create bright necklaces and bracelets to wear when school started next week.

Mom parted Betsy's thick, coarse hair into a section the size for a roller, soaked it and a curling tissue with the correct chemical, and rolled the hair tight to Betsy's skull. Cat picked that moment to walk through, size up the situation, and snort.

"Who cares about curls?" she scoffed. "I'm going to find myself a game of marbles. Or do something useful like making sure that stray dog's doing okay with his new family. He's got two little boys to play with there." With that, she flaunted her honey-blonde pigtails tied in emerald green ribbon.

The door slammed, and of course Mom made her come back and leave again, this time closing the door quietly.

"Little sisters," Betsy said, shaking her head. Both Fran and Mary Beth had older siblings, but no young ones to pester and tease them. Some people have all the luck, Betsy told herself for about the hundredth time this week. It had been a long summer putting up with Cat.

"I'm signing up to sell savings stamps at school this year," Mary Beth said, her smile showing off the dimple in her left cheek. "Are you?"

"Sure thing," Fran and Betsy chimed in.

"I want to help with the school paper, too," Betsy added.

"Count me in on working with every scrap drive," Fran said, smoothing her new pageboy hairstyle.

"Isn't it swell that we'll be in the high school building this year?" Betsy tucked in her chin so Mom could roll a curler at the nape of her neck.

"And getting a bunch of new kids, too, coming in from Timnath and Severance." Fran dipped the brush into a bottle of bright red nail polish and began applying it to the large wishbone she held in her left hand. When the polish dried, she'd take a strand of red or white yarn and string it into a necklace. They'd slide their colored macaroni in different lengths for bracelets and necklaces.

"I hope there's some cute boys," Mary Beth said.

The girls giggled and a stream of chatter followed – What dress are you going to wear? Did you get new saddle shoes or penny loafers? I hope Mrs. Tabor is teaching Latin. Sure is too bad Mr. Phillips got drafted. I've got a great idea for a Student Council project – if I get elected. Let's sign up to pick potatoes together during harvest break. It had better be in a place not anywhere close to a sugar beet field full of P.O.W.s.

The room fell silent.

"Now, girls," Mom said, "don't borrow trouble. Just keep reminding yourselves you're helping with the war effort."

~

At supper that evening Dad thanked Mom for the good meal, admired the bounce in Betsy's hair, then said, "Let's get the kitchen cleared and drive out and work in the Victory Garden. Plenty of hoeing and weeding and irrigating to do. The best part comes last – tomatoes, cucumbers, carrots, string beans, and sweet corn just ripe enough to pick and bring home."

Betsy wanted to go but worried what digging in the dirt would do to her new perm. "Gee, Dad, I . . . . ," she stammered, glancing at Mom.

"Your perm's lovely, Betsy," Mom said, "gardening won't hurt it. Wrap a bandana over that new hairdo and it'll be fine."

"Forget being beautiful," Cat said with the hint of a sneer. "Sweet corn – yum!" Cat said, patting her mid-section. "Sure wish we had butter, though."

The Blakeslys had voted unanimously – none of that white margarine that came with a big dot of yellow coloring to blend with the margarine and pretend it was butter. For them it was butter or nothing.

The sugar factory had assigned plots of ground at the edge of their property for people to plant Victory Gardens. Dad, a staunch meat, potatoes, and gravy man, had thrown himself into gardening to the point where he'd even planted – and was eating – vegetables he would never have tasted before, like bell peppers, broccoli, and acorn squash. As they weeded and hoed, they talked – about their relatives in the military, about the latest war news, about the weather, about their latest trip to Denver, and about – the prisoner of war camp and the trainloads of prisoners arriving.

~

Early Monday morning after he finished his coffee, Dad kissed them one by one, grabbed his cap, and rolled up the sleeves of his blue work shirt. "Should be interesting at the factory today. They're bringing in a few of the prisoners who've just arrived at the camp. Maybe I'll get a chance to practice all that German I took in high school and college."

He went out the door whistling *"Yankee Doodle Dandy"* off tune.

"Mom," Betsy said, her eyes fixing on her mother's, "is Dad really going to talk to those Nazis?"

"Nobody can beat up on my daddy." Billie scowled.

"Of course not. He knows how to take care of himself," Cat agreed, with the hint of a quiver in her voice.

"Listen, children," Mom explained, "remember that the prisoners are here to help out on the farms. The farmers can't get the crops harvested without more help than we have available, now that all our own young people are gone. Meanwhile it's up to us to do the best we can and get on with our lives."

Betsy helped clear the table and stack the dishes, reminded Cat it was her turn for dishwashing duty, then reviewed her list of deliveries before heading out on her last full week of business. When school started, she'd still do a few errands after school and on Saturdays when she could, but officially this was her last week. She'd miss seeing her customers, but she had to admit it would be a relief not to knock on Mrs. Slipher's door and listen to her endless complaints. Another thing, too – her bike tires were wearing so thin she was always getting a flat. Still, she didn't know how she'd manage to do deliveries without her bike. Between mechanically minded Jack and Dad's friend who'd built her bike three years ago, they'd repaired the damage Spud and his gang did, she used it every day.

Turning onto Main Street, she heard the rumble of a farm truck. Strange, she thought, farmers always picked up their workers just before dawn. The truck soon drew parallel with her and as it passed ahead, in the truck bed she saw rows of men dressed alike in blue denim uniforms. Prisoners of war.

And then she found herself gazing into the face of one of them – young, maybe as young as she was, his blue eyes open wide like those of a frightened deer.

CHAPTER 6

Help the War Effort

"Hippity-hop to the barbershop," Billie sang, his eyes focused on the fat red-and-white stripes of the barber's pole.

Without warning he stumbled, pitching forward. Betsy caught him and stood him upright.

Titters and muffled giggles sounded from the dark space between a pair of buildings. The fat stick that had tripped Billie disappeared. Betsy's jaw clenched. Spud Sherman and his gang. What would he be up to next?

"Come along, Billie," she said, looking straight ahead, hurried toward Clyde Willowby's shop a couple of doors away. The sidewalk shimmered waves hot enough to crack open one of Cat's hen's eggs and fry it. She pictured herself smashing Spud Sherman's freckled face into the yolk.

They pushed inside the shop. Almost as hot inside despite the ceiling fan's efforts, but being inside calmed Betsy with its familiar sounds and smells. The banter of men, the slaps of the shoeshine boy's polishing rag, the barber pumping the chair up or down with his foot, spinning the chair around, shoes walking across the black and white checkered floor, all blended with the smells shaving cream and after shave lotion, shoe polish, cigar smoke, and men, mostly Main Street businessmen along with Wayne from the gas station and Hank Schiff, who farmed east of town. Joey Sullivan's shoeshine customer blew smoke rings in the air. Joey glanced up and smiled, then went back to his job.

Clyde nodded at Billie. "Be with you soon, Master Blakesly."

To Betsy he said, "Sure do miss cutting your hair. Best kind for the bobbed cut. But I suppose now that you're in high school, you want to be like the other girls...." His voice trailed off as he busied himself with shaving the man in the chair – wrapped in the billowing black-and-white striped apron, chair tipped back, face slathered with shaving cream.

Betsy smiled at Clyde, remembering the feel of the chair being pumped up, the paper tissue around her neck, Clyde's chatter and teasing as he snipped away.

"I'm not a little girl anymore. And hair fashions change," she pointed out. "Now the rage is pompadours and page boys, hair tucked inside colored snoods, Veronica Lake's wave cascading over one eye."

Clyde lifted the curved razor, wiped it clean, tested the thin blade, traced it across the cheek again, holding the flesh steady with his left hand. Betsy shivered. What if the razor slipped? She pictured blood streaming. That's when she noticed the customer's shoes – brown-and-white men's spectators – and knew the man was Harvey P. Slipher. The only man in town who wore them. Maybe she wouldn't mind seeing a few drops of blood appear.

Pete Taylor, the druggist, signaled Betsy and Billie to sit next to him on the gleaming dark wood bench that faced the two barber stations. Two stations, one barber. Clyde's partner had gone off to war.

The barber covered his customer's face with a hot, wet towel, wiped his hands on his apron, and winked at Billie. "Shave and a haircut today, young feller?"

Billie giggled and squirmed.

Pete Taylor ruffled Billie's thick brown hair. "How about giving me some of that hair? Cover up that bald spot I've acquired."

Billie looked at the shiny spot.

"And would you believe it?" He shot the barber a look. "That man snipping the scissors still charges me the full two bits."

"Look at the advantages, Pete," Clyde said, punctuating his words with a wave of his black comb. "You don't have to stand in front of the mirror parting a bunch of hair just so, rubbing in hair oil, then combing it in place like some folks do."

Clyde cranked the chair upright and got on with the haircut.

Pete turned to the man on the other side of Billie. "So, Hank," he said, "gonna have enough manpower to get those beets out?"

Hank ran his fingers around the brim of his straw hat and nodded. "Could make it, all right. The way they're moving prisoners into the camp, we'll have some pretty strong backs out there in the fields. And there's rumors the factory's trucking in Mexican nationals. And we've got help coming from the Mexican colony outside of town."

Betsy had seen whole families of Mexicans working in the fields, not just the men.

Pete held up his first two fingers in the "V" for victory sign.

"'Course, we still need the town folks pitching in." Hank glanced at Betsy. "Including all those young folks with strong backs from school. Every single one!"

Betsy swelled inside. Getting the harvest in meant food for the troops.

"I'll open the shop just two days a week during harvest," Clyde announced. "Help with weighing beets prob'ly. Except for Sundays." He let his words sink in. "Folks may have to start making appointments to get their hair cut."

Pete Taylor said he'd mind his pharmacy afternoons. Mornings were for helping the farmers. He was short of help, too, and had hired two housewives to stock shelves and wait on customers along with a couple of teenagers behind the soda fountain.

Mr. Slipher squirmed. Clyde's hand hiccupped and a trickle of blood appeared on his customer's ear lobe. He let out a yip. Clyde froze.

"Watch it, Clyde," the Plains Picture Show owner/funeral parlor director, growled. "You could have sliced off my ear!"

The room fell silent and no one looked at anyone else, except for Billie whose eyes went back and forth from one man to the other. Nearly bursting beneath the silence was a hint of stifled laughter.

"Well, just a little nick, Harvey. No harm done," Clyde said, cleaning the drop of blood with a neck tissue. "And you were about to say...."

The wounded man sat up straight. "Of course I'll do my share, but as you know, I have heavy business demands. I'll have to sacrifice to cut an hour or two off the work week. Besides, I need to be choosy about how I help. I won't crawl on my hands and knees in a field, and you won't catch me anywhere near those Krauts! Where's all this business of foreigners in our midst going to end? We've already got all those Rooshuns in Mill Town that go to that church where they speak German. Time they learned to talk American."

"Back off, Harvey," Pete said. "You know they're experienced and hard workers in sugar beet fields. They're doing their best in a strange country with a strange language. I've hired a couple of school kids who live on that side of town, and I can tell you they've had good upbringing. And I might add that every cent they earn they hand over to their fathers."

The man in the chair muttered something and changed the subject. "Thank heaven we don't have any of those Jap internment camps close by or we'd have an invasion of horse-toothed, yellow-skinned, slant-eyes, too. No other governor but our Governor Carr would let those enemy spies step their big toe over their state line."

One of Betsy's church school papers had a story about what life was like for a girl her age in one of those camps. She'd shuddered and thought how horrid it was to take American citizens away from their homes and their lush gardens on the west coast and treat them like they were prisoners of war, too. Worse yet, their young men were drafted into the Army like all American boys. It was so confusing. So unjust.

The barber whisked the hair off his customer's neck, untied the strings and gathered up the apron. "You're all dandied up, Harvey," Clyde said. "So you can get on back to the movie theatre or your mortuary, whichever place you're taking care of today."

Clyde held up the hand mirror. Mr. Slipher studied his reflection, pointed out a few stray hairs for Clyde to clip, then tightened his polka dot bow tie, called back, "Put it on my bill," and left the shop in a huff. The bell on the door jangled.

Suddenly the air felt lighter and even cooler. Clyde slid the board across the arms of the barber chair and lifted Billie up. Joey Sullivan's customer handed him a quarter. Pete Taylor took the empty seat and placed his worn brown leather shoe on the polishing stand. Maybe when the next rationing books were issued, Betsy thought, he'd buy a new pair.

The good-natured rhythm of men's voices resumed and Betsy, sighing, leaned back on the bench.

On the way home, she glanced in the window of the Coffee Cup Café, noted the three dollar lunch special for the day: choice of tomato or orange juice, meatloaf, mashed potatoes, peas, homemade rolls and butter, fruit cocktail and choice of tea, coffee, or milk. A pair of small black and white signs in the corner of the door said, *"Whites Only"* and *"Talk American."* She'd never noticed those signs before. Maybe because the Blakeslys, like most families, hardly ever thought about eating anywhere but in their own kitchen or dining room.

CHAPTER 7

Nothing Can Stop the Army Air Corps

After a hurried Spam and sweet pickle sandwich at home, Betsy joined Rosemary at the Savings Stamps sales booth outside the principal's office. Students – boys dressed in cream-colored cords, plaid cotton shirts, and saddle shoes, books in one hand at their side; girls in trim skirts and sloppy Joe sweaters, hugging their books with both arms – called to one another, opened and slammed shut their locker doors, bumped elbows and shoulders. Some stood in line to sign up for the next War Bond, scrap metal, rubber, and paper drives. Others talked among themselves as they waited at the Savings Stamps booth, dimes in their pockets or coin purses. Betsy was getting close to having enough stamp books filled to trade it in for a $25 War Bond – after the war, she'd cash every bond she bought to help pay for college. Every $25 dollars would help, even if only a little bit.

Betsy and Rosemary wasted no time taking care of their customers. The bell for fifth period would soon ring. Storing the sheets of stamps and stamp books away, they poured the cash into the heavy green bag and turned it over to the school secretary. Mrs. Greene beamed, impressed by how many stamps they'd sold, then locked the money in the safe and shooed the girls off to class.

Latin II. Ugh. Not the best class to walk into right after lunch. Her brain worked better in the morning. Why not girls' p.e.? Then they could play softball or run around the track and forget about books and pop quizzes for a while. She sure was glad that band came last. They'd go out on the football field to practice the half-time drills for Friday night's game. No break from books in her schedule this period, though. It was Latin. Conjugations, declensions, and vocabulary weren't so bad. It was the translations that gave her trouble.

Striding along beside Rosemary, arms wrapped around notebook and texts, Betsy nearly lost her balance when someone pushed against her. Rosemary steadied her and glared at the offender.

"You're blocking the hall," Colleen Sherman called, tossing her long auburn curls, not even glancing back. She wasn't carrying her books. Blackie Hoffman was, hers along with his.

Rosemary frowned, turned to Betsy. "Hummph. Wearing Blackie's letter sweater – she sure thinks she's Somebody."

"I wonder how she bribes her bratty brother not to tattle."

Everyone knew that if the Shermans found out their daughter had a crush on a fellow from the other side of the tracks, they wouldn't let Colleen out of their sight.

Mrs. Frei was just closing the door when Betsy and Rosemary slipped inside the classroom to the ring of the tardy bell.

Betsy sighed as she settled into her seat. She hated to admit it, but Blackie and Colleen were a swell-looking couple – muscular Blackie, a senior, with his coal black curls and sun-browned skin were the perfect contrast with Colleen's silken complexion lightly sprinkled with freckles, striking green-blue eyes, and graceful figure. Oh, well, she told herself, in Colleen's case, "Beauty is only skin deep."

~

The minute she stepped through the kitchen door, she knew something was wrong. Mom, Cat, and Billie were at the table, an after-school snack waiting – crisp Jonathan apple slices, graham crackers with peanut butter, a pitcher of cold milk. Mom motioned Betsy to take her usual place. What was happening?

Mom took a deep breath. "This afternoon," she began, looking round at each of them, "your Uncle Ben phoned Dad to tell him he'd just gotten a telegram."

Betsy's heart skipped a beat. Long distance calls were saved for evening or weekend rates. And family calls to Dad at the factory were not allowed. She could tell Mom was trying hard to keep her voice steady.

"About Johnny?" Cat whispered Betsy's question. When had Cat ever been known to lower her voice to a *whisper.*

Mom nodded. "About Johnny. But don't worry. He isn't wounded. Or killed."

"What then?" Betsy breathed.

"He's been reported 'Missing in Action.' It seems his plane was shot down in enemy territory. It will take time before they know what's happened to him. "

"But, Mom," Betsy said, pleading, "they've just got to find him. And how do we know for sure that he wasn't wounded or killed in the crash? Or captured?"

The four of them sat looking at one another. What could anyone say?

The song *"Comin' In On a Wing and a Prayer"* started playing inside Betsy's head. Maybe the plane crash hadn't been too awful. Maybe his plane had come in on a wing and prayer and Johnny was hiding out in daylight hours, crawling under cover of night to find his way out of enemy fire. She'd seen scenes like that in the newsreels and between the covers of *Life* magazine. Maybe, maybe that's what was happening.

Shreds of peanut butter and graham cracker spit out with Billie's words. "Hitler can't get Johnny. He's got brains – and and and he's sooo – brave!"

Cat patted Billie's hand. "You bet he is! He'll come home safe. I know it!"

Mom's shoulders relaxed and her face softened with a small smile. "That's the ticket," she said. "So let's have our snack. It's our responsibility to stay strong and healthy, too, you know."

Cat and Billie ran outside to play. Betsy pounded out the Army Air Corps song on the piano three times before going into the kitchen where Mom was lining up pots and lids.

"How can I go to the game tonight, Mom? I mean, knowing about Johnny and...." She began peeling the potatoes Mom had set out next to the sink.

"What would Johnny want you to do, Betsy. What would he want all of us to do."

Betsy blinked back the tears in her eyes, cut the potato into quarters and dropped them into the pan of cold water.

"I suppose," she said at last, "he'd want us to be brave. He'd want us to just keep going. But, Mom, is this war ever going to end?"

"Only if all of us keep doing our part to support our boys. So you need to put on that band uniform and walk on over to Emily's for the pre-game chili supper like always." She cupped Betsy's chin in her hand. "Remember. If we don't keep our spirits up, the enemy wins."

"Okay. Sure. But I hope Dad gets home in time to tie my tie!" She forced a smile. "I'd never pass inspection if I tried to tie it myself."

Dad was talking with Mom in the kitchen when Betsy came out dressed in her gray-blue band uniform and holding her tie. Dad's tie. Like the white starched shirt she borrowed from him, too.

He took both ends of the tie, positioned it under the shirt collar, and began the process of wrapping the correct knot. "Bad news about Johnny, Kiddo," he said, tightening the knot and sliding it up. "Still, it could be much worse, so the best we can do is hope and pray. Promise?"

He looked her in the eye. She gulped and said, "Promise."

"And keep on sending those V-mails to him! When he makes it back to base, there'll be a bagful of letters from home to welcome him. And we need to send letters often to Uncle Ben and Aunt Louise."

She lifted her head and nodded, then pointed at the tie. "Thanks for making sure I pass inspection." Strange how wearing her band uniform made her feel so soldiery, but it did and she kept those brass buttons polished to a shine.

Dad clicked his heels together and saluted, set her hat in place, handed her the saxophone case, then looked at her saddle shoes and said, "And an 'A+' for your saddle shoes. Spotless." *(Betsy winced. Everybody wore dirty saddle shoes. Except her. Shined shoes was a number one rule of Dad's. Why couldn't she be like the other kids?)* He held the door and ushered her out. "So, Miss Betsy Blakesly, march on and cheer those Warriors of ours on to win!"

She called good-bye and promised to come right home after the game.

"Hey, Big Sis, see ya there!" Cat said.

Not if she could help it, Betsy vowed silently. At least Cat and her friends would be at the far end of the stands in the junior high section.

On her way out, Betsy glanced at Dad's air raid warden hat on the hook next to the back porch door. A shiver rippled down her spine.

CHAPTER 8

Two Million More Women Needed

T he *Rocky Mountain News* said it in their morning edition, *The Denver Post* headlined it in the evening, and this week's *Sun* would probably announce it, too: *Two Million More Women Needed in War Plants.* Every day more men were leaving their lathes and forges to serve in the military – and the ones holding 4-F draft cards had to take on the work of two or more men. That left it to women to take over those kinds of jobs. Women like her friend Emily Mason's sister working in a war plant on the west coast.

Betsy sighed. Too young to work in a war plant, too young to join the Red Cross, too young to enlist in the Women's Air Corps, too young. The words read like headlines in Betsy's head. She was nothing but a "bobby-soxer." She steered her bike onto Main Street.

"Betsy – wait a sec, okay?"

Emily pulled alongside her on her blue bike with balloon tires, reached out and gave Betsy's arm a little squeeze. "I'm so sorry about Johnny," she said.

Betsy forced a smile. "Thanks, Em."

They were quiet a while then, not saying the words but each knowing the other's thoughts.

Em broke the silence. "If this is a packages from home day, I'd like to help, okay?"

Betsy's shoulders relaxed and she gave Emily a grateful smile. "Gee thanks, kid, that would be swell."

Across the street Fred Hopper was painting more names on the Honor Roll board. He didn't need the ladder today. These were the last ones in the last column on the board.

One of them, Danny Zeigler, should be in this year's senior class, but he'd missed a year of school to help on his dad's farm. That made him old enough to be drafted. Now he was in boot camp.

Fred looked up and put his brush in the can of blue paint. "Packages from home day?" he called.

They biked across. Betsy nodded. "Can't send them as often now, what with such a big list and sugar and Crisco in shorter supply almost every week."

Emily pointed to the board. "No more spaces, Fred. Where will the next names go?"

"Hate to say it," Fred said, shaking his head, "but we're adding a new panel right next to this one."

"Mighty good game our Warriors played last night," Fred said, changing the subject. "Good coaching, good team work, good spirit in the stands – led of course by our cheerleaders and marching band. Hats off to you two horn blowers!"

"A heart-breaker, though. Imagine how Herb must have felt when his kick veered off to the side." Emily shook her head.

"I'd hate to be the one who had to make the winning point," Betsy added. She thought of how she felt before a piano recital. All cold and trembly. What if she sat with her hands poised above the keys and her mind went blank? Or if she got stuck at the place that always gave her trouble and she couldn't go on? Or if her fingers hit a G flat instead of that G sharp? And there was Herb with the stands full of fans holding their breath, his teammates and coach – all expecting him to make that one single point.

"Nerves," Fred said as if he could read Betsy's mind. "Normal enough and healthy in moderation. Coach'll help him stay more calm next game. But time you two got those care packages down to the post office, and me to tend to my own business."

Riding past the movie theatre, Betsy read the marquee – another movie with Bob Hope, Bing Crosby, and Dorothy Lamour. Next week was Fred Astaire and Ginger Rogers. Betsy had a crush on Van Johnson, and she had to admit his co-star June Allyson was a perfect match. The kid sweeping the sidewalk kicked at a rock, the corners of his mouth turned down.

"I'd bet a dime Mr. Slipher's got that poor kid scared out of his skin. He's way too young to work for anyone," Emily said, "but Mr. Slipher...."

"A million dollars couldn't persuade me to work for him." Betsy pushed down hard on her pedals and clenched her teeth all the way to the Newsoms' kitchen door.

"Oh, good, Betsy," Mrs. Newsom said, welcoming the girls in, "you've brought Emily along to help."

"She volunteered for duty," Betsy said, taking one of the chairs Mrs. Sundstrom pulled out. Mrs. Sundstrom 's face glowed and from more than the heat of the oven. The Sundstroms had just gotten V-mails from both their sons.

Mrs. Taylor finished addressing the last package, then slid a plate of cookies toward the girls. Pouring milk into the glass in front of Betsy, she said, "We're so sorry to hear the news about your cousin, Betsy." Mrs. Newsom gave her a quick hug and murmurs of "Surely he'll come home safe" came from each of the three women.

Mrs. Newsom looked at Emily. "And what do you hear from your brother, Ed – and your sister out there in that war plant in California?"

After exchanging pleasantries, Mrs. Taylor's expression changed and she told the girls that someone had thrown rotten eggs at the drugstore door during the night and chalked things like "Hun-lover" and "... you call yourself patriotic?!" all over the plate glass windows. Her husband, Pete, had hired a boy to help him clean up the mess, but they wouldn't be able to erase the bitter taste of what lurked behind the act.

"Do they know who did it?" Emily asked.

The ladies looked at one another, then one of them said, "Pete has his suspicions, but he won't say."

Betsy remembered back to that day she and Billie waited in Clyde's barbershop and called up her own suspicions. She wouldn't put it past Mr. Slipher to get somebody to do the vandalizing.

Mrs. Newsom wiped her hands on her apron and drew in her breath. "Well, we're about to let ourselves in for some hate tricks," she said and turned to Betsy and Emily.

"And I'm sorry to bring you girls into it, but I need you."

Betsy and Emily looked at one another, then chorused, "Of course we'll help if we can."

"Doc Wendling told us about a few P.O.W.s he's treating in the infirmary out there. He says they're good boys, not the SS kind, and besides being sick, they're very lonesome for home. Thought some home baked goodies might cheer them up."

Mrs. Sundstrom rushed to explain. "So we've got cinnamon rolls ready for the oven and need you to take them out to the camp." She paused and went on. "Doc arranged it with the commander in charge. They'll open the gate for you."

"And I've asked Jack Gordon to drive you out when he gets off work at the bakery. He'll pick you up here at four o'clock."

Biking the packages onto Main Street, Betsy looked at Emily. "Us? Take cinnamon rolls to the prisoners?"

Emily returned the look. "What did we just get ourselves into? Hey, maybe we could just attach a note saying 'Kilroy was here.'"

They staggered under the load of brown paper wrapped boxes, their eyes looking straight ahead at the poster of an American flag printed with the words *"Give It Your Best!"* on the post office wall.

Back at the Newsoms' house Jack was placing the cinnamon rolls on the floor of the car's back seat. Hearing the girls approach, he called, "Train's leaving. Jump on board," and he hurried to open the passenger door.

CHAPTER 9

Don't Fence Me In

"Your dad's sure swell to let you use the car, Jack." Emily leaned forward from her seat next to the window, Betsy in the middle, Jack driving – plenty of space for all three, but Betsy had to squeeze her knees to the right of the stick shift. She hated to admit it, but Jack's knack for knowing just how to ease the clutch out so the car didn't jerk ahead made her few attempts at that skill look just plain stupid. But he'd had his driver's license for several months now. Experienced compared to her. She'd worry about that when she turned sixteen and gas rationing ended along with the war.

They'd passed through town and now Main Street's black top ended. The Gordons' black Chevy sedan was on the gravel road leading outside the city limits. Betsy's stomach knotted. Every turn of the wheels took them closer to the prison camp.

Outside the city limits the road meandered through a shabby stretch – Mexican colony, junk yard, scattered tumbledown shacks, unkempt yards, scrawny cats and dogs, a handful of goats searching for scraps where the goat lady lived in some kind of shelter made of cardboard boxes and slabs of discarded aluminum. Betsy wondered what her life was like.

"Dad's okay," Jack said, then grinned. "The promise of an extra big cinnamon roll for him may have done the trick." He breathed in the aroma of freshly baked bread. "Gosh, I could eat the whole pan!"

"There'll be one waiting for each of us when we get back," Betsy reminded him. To herself she added, *If* we get back. In her imagination she pictured one of those Doberman watchdogs taking a chunk out of her leg, a Nazi prisoner glaring at her, maybe getting locked inside that fence.

Determined not to get cold feet, she studied the scene on the other side of the city limits. "Not exactly a good first impression for people driving into Plainsview."

"Oh, oh, I smell a project cooking up in Miss Blakesly's brain." Jack shot Em a knowing look.

Em nodded. "Forget it, Betsy. Cleaning up that stretch is not any of our business. Maybe that's how they like it. Besides the war effort comes first."

That doesn't mean we couldn't bring up the subject to whoever's in charge, Betsy said to herself but dropped the subject. They chattered about school, band practice, last week's football game. Much too soon they reached the place where the landscape changed to a wide curve approaching the hill where they'd watched the camp going up all summer. Betsy swept that thought away and pointed to the grove of shade trees on the other side of the road, their leaves turning from shades of velvet green to shimmering gold and orange. "That old barn's not going to make it through the winter," she commented, wondering how long it had been abandoned. The paint was gone, the entire barn leaned at a precarious angle, shingles were missing from the roof. "I wonder whose it is?"

"And in such a pretty meadow, too," Em added. "What a shame."

"Not sure who owns that land," Jack said, squinting. The sun was at its brightest before it began its descent behind the purple-colored twin peaks.

But now the car was climbing the hill. Watchtowers on the east side of the road rose into view against the horizon. Betsy and Emily clutched hands.

Then Jack turned off the main road and down the drive leading to the prison gates. Betsy's breath caught. Suddenly the watchtowers loomed like giant monsters with cavernous eyes, beacon lights attached to their heads, guns like arms of steel protruding. The series of barracks stretched wide and long over what used to be Sam Albertson's potato field. Prisoners and armed guards were walking about, the watchdogs snarling along that barbed-wire fence stretched higher than Betsy could have imagined. The dogs curled their lips exposing sharp fangs, their eyes shooting sparks, hair on their necks laid back.

Betsy froze in place, felt Em freeze, too.

Jack pulled the car close, braked, and turned off the engine. He looked at the girls, must have known they were scared. "Hey, there's nothing to be afraid of," he said as if entering a prisoner of war camp were an everyday occurrence. "We're not walking past the gate. The guard will open it, Betsy you hand him the rolls, and we drive off. Nothing to it, okay?"

Nothing to it, my left foot, Betsy said to herself, feeling her legs turn to jelly. She sure didn't want to see any of them face to face.

And then the gate swung open, an American soldier with sergeant first class stripes on his sleeve stepped out, took one look at Jack and wrung his hand. "Imagine meeting me here, Jack," he said, a wide smile spreading across his ruddy face.

"Bill! I'd heard you were here! This is one for Ripley's *'Believe It Or Not'* column!"

Betsy let her shoulders relax a little. It was Bill Hoff, all right! She'd only seen him a couple of times before when he'd been home on leave from the European front. Now they'd stationed him here.

"Feels like I just got demoted, to tell the truth," he was saying to Jack. "Look at me – back home instead of over there on the lines with my buddies. Some hot shot claims they need me to talk German to the prisoners so they don't try to pull anything on the guards who don't understand German. Hmmm. Just my luck."

Bill's birth name was Wilhelm, but that didn't sound American, so he'd changed it to "Bill." His parents had come to sugar beet land with others from the settlement of Germans from Russia. Like all children in these families who'd emigrated from their German settlement on the Volga River, Bill had grown up speaking German and still did at home. When he'd started first grade, he learned English in a hurry.

Jack shook his head. "I can only imagine what a slap that would be," he said, then paused. "But one thing's sure – we sure feel safer knowing you're keeping these prisoners in line."

Betsy handed him the pan of rolls. "For the fellows in sick bay, compliments of Plainsview packages from home committee – Doc Wendling's prescription."

"They sure smell good! Cooks here aren't exactly famous for serving up home-style grub. Please give the ladies our thanks, Betsy." He clicked his heels and saluted.

Betsy! She felt a little thrill. He'd remembered her name!

"And Emily," Bill said, looking past Betsy. "You're in on this, too. The fellas are gonna cheer up in a hurry. Thanks to the three of you for going beyond the call of duty...but don't be surprised if you catch flack from some of the town folks when word gets out about this."

Jack shrugged. "Make sure you help yourself to at least one of those rolls, Bill. Orders from cooks' headquarters."

They called good-byes, heard the heavy gate close then lock behind them, and drove back to Plainsview, not talking. Betsy kept thinking of her cousin Johnny, wondering what German soldiers like the ones at the camp here could have done to him. Killed him? Taken him prisoner? Tortured him? Wasn't that what they were trained to do?

She pictured those Nazi soldiers on war posters, in magazines, newspapers, newsreels – goose-stepping, armed, faceless. But then another picture rose from her memory... that first farm truck taking prisoners out to the field, the lost look on the face of a boy who couldn't have been older than she was.

She couldn't wait to get home. To sit down to supper with her family. To feel that life was – normal.

CHAPTER 10

Justice for All

The windows were raised as high as they could go, but still the room felt stuffy with mid-day heat and smells of chalk dust mingling with that of forty some sophomores jammed into a room meant for no more than thirty. Some kids shared desks, a few leaned with their backs against the radiator next to the open windows. Chuck, class president, pushed the agenda to its final items. They needed to adjourn before lunch hour ended, the only time in the school day bus students could attend club or class meetings.

"Let's see the victory sign," he said, "sophomores collected the most scrap this month – paper, scrap metal, old rubber, the works – check the chart outside the main office if you haven't already." He waited for cheers and right hands raised in a "V."

He paused and went on. "Seniors took first place on sales of savings stamps, and juniors tied with us for the number of letters sent to servicemen and women."

A shriek pierced the air. Heads turned. "Get him away from me!" Colleen Sherman screamed, waving her arms around aimlessly. The bee buzzed next to her ear lobe.

Ruthie got up from across the aisle, swatted the bee, and squashed it on the floor with the heel of her shoe. Colleen resumed her queenly pose. Titters of laughter rippled across the room. Chuck called for attention.

Kids were getting restless, glancing at the big wall clock behind the teacher's desk. Someone tapped a pencil, shoes shuffled against the wood floor. Mrs. Frei, class sponsor, who'd been standing at the back of the room, began wandering up and down the aisles, arms folded against her beige dress. Betsy tried to signal Chuck not to call on her, but she couldn't catch his eye. Her heart raced. Why, oh why, had she ever brought up such a dumb idea? It was the wrong time, the wrong topic, the wrong everything.

Chuck rapped the small gavel. "I know time's nearly up, but we have an item of new business to bring up first. Betsy will explain what it's about, and I'm asking that you listen but not comment. That's for another meeting. Are the rules clear? – Listen, but no talk."

Low grumbling and mumbling rippled, covert frowns cast toward Betsy. Her spirit sank. She'd already been snubbed by certain people after word got out about the visit to the prison camp. Now here she was asking for more. She felt the familiar flush of awkward embarrassment on her face. No, she couldn't do it.

Then she thought again. . . she'd promised herself to do this for Johnny's sake, for Hal Martin, her uncle, all the ones whose names she knew and those she didn't know. She'd talked it over with some of her friends as well as with Mom and Dad, and they had encouraged her. Even Cat and Billie had cheered her on. Okay, she told herself. She'd do it. No matter what Colleen Sherman and others thought or said or did.

Chuck beckoned. "Please come to the front of the room, Betsy, so everyone can hear."

Somehow she got to the front of the room, sensing forty pairs of eyes burning holes in her back with every step she took. The note card in her hand shook. She steadied it with her other hand and took a deep breath. Chuck gave her an encouraging pat on the shoulder. Mrs. Frei nodded approval.

Betsy glanced at her notes. "As Chuck has just announced," she said, her voice quivering a little, "we're all of us – every single one – working hard for the war effort. And we know from letters we've gotten from our local servicemen and women that everything we do does make a difference. A big difference." She looked at Mary Beth sitting in the back row. Mary Beth beamed, giving her courage to go on.

"Every American is fighting to hold onto freedom and justice for all," Betsy paused, swallowed her nervousness, and plunged ahead. "But when you think about it, does everyone really truly have freedom? One example is that even in our small town of 2,000, the few of us whose skin color is dark do not have the freedom to walk through the door of the Coffee Cup Café or sit on the main floor at the movies or swim in the public pool."

She could almost feel the temperature climb in the room, heard the sucking in of breaths, an undertow of murmurs. Chuck nudged her, said, "You're doing fine, Betsy. You're doing fine."

She swallowed hard again. "So it seems to me that while our people in the service are fighting with tanks and bombs and guns overseas, we could fight a war without weapons right here in our town to make freedom a reality for all citizens. Maybe we could take it on as an optional class project."

"Okay," Chuck said, taking over the meeting again, "Betsy's presented us with an idea. One worth study and thought. Who will volunteer to serve on a committee to research the idea, present us with their findings, and make a proposal either in favor of or against accepting it as a project."

The silence in the room thundered in Betsy's ears. And then someone's hand shot in the air.

"I'll volunteer." Willie! The class clown who wiggles his Mickey Mouse ears.

Betsy nearly gasped. Who would have thought Willie would raise his hand?

"That's one," Chuck counted. "Could we have three more?"

Half a dozen hands or more went up. Chuck grinned and pointed to three others – "Rosemary, Leland, and Glenn. Swell. That makes a committee of five. Betsy, you call them together and get started. We'll expect a report at our next meeting."

Everyone was looking around at each other. Betsy was trying to take it all in.

"Is there a motion for adjournment?" Chuck asked. "A second? All in favor? Meeting adjourned."

"Good job, Betsy," Chuck said as they moved to leave.

Mrs. Frei stood at the door, making sure students left in orderly fashion.

Emily grasped Betsy's hand, Mary Beth coming alongside them.

"You did it, Kid, you did it."

Out in the hall, Colleen muttered loud enough for others to hear, "I suppose next you'll not only have us taking treats to the Nazis but making room for them at the cafe, taking the best seats at the movies."

A boy's voice behind her chimed in with "And them niggers in Denver'll move in, too."

A sour taste rose on Betsy's tongue. She bit her lip and hurried to her locker. Whatever she'd let herself in for was sure to bring trouble. And yet – people had actually volunteered for the committee. The bad taste dissolved. Maybe she wasn't the only one who believed in this, after all.

~

At supper that evening (the usual Spam but doctored with pineapple, acorn squash and the last of the string beans from the victory garden, with fresh raspberries from the backyard over a scoop of creamy vanilla ice cream from Jud's soda fountain) they first ate in silence during Edward R. Murrow's news broadcast, intent on hearing the latest developments in the war. The fighting had grown even more intense on the European front, and then there were the battles raging in North Africa, Italy, and maybe worst of all in the Pacific. Hitler, Mussolini, Hiro Hito – *who was the cruelest?*

After the broadcast, Dad lightened the mood with a story about what it was like having young college age girls instead of men or boys working alongside him in the factory's lab. "They're as sweet and bright as a pure crystal of sugar," he said. He'd claimed more than once that women were better and stronger than men, and now he was having that proven every day of the sugar campaign season.

"Of course they are, Daddy," Cat said. "And since they're so smart, how about having them conduct some experiments in finding a better substitute for ham than Spam?" She looked at Mom. "Sorry, Mom, but I'm sick and tired of Spam."

"Me, too," Billie agreed, and carefully set each bite of Spam on his plate onto the rim.

"Now see what you've done, Carol," Mom said. "Billie, you clean up your plate just like the rest of us. We're lucky to have Spam to eat."

Dad swallowed the last bite of his squash and looked at Betsy. "So, Sis, how did the class meeting go? Did they boo or cheer your idea?"

Billie jumped up and down. "I bet they clapped and cheered!"

"I can guess what Colleen Sherman did," Cat said, screwing up her face.

Mom hushed them, saying, "If you'll stop talking, then Betsy can tell us."

The sun was setting when the fire siren shrilled and the church bells rang. Dad laid his napkin next to his plate and headed for the back door, grabbing his air raid warden's hat and paraphernalia. Mom, Cat, and Betsy hurried to pull the blackout curtains tight, Billie switched off the lights, and the four of them huddled together on the big davenport in the living room, a supply of candles and matches resting on the coffee table.

No one said what they were thinking. What if this turned out to be the real thing? What if someone out there – an escaped P.O.W. – would grab Dad and hurt him? What if – ? The "what ifs" never ended.

Billie piped up in a scared voice, "Mom, tell about the time we had our summer vacation at the cabin by the Big Thompson River."

And so the story-telling went on till the siren and bells signaled the "All Clear" and they breathed big sighs of relief, turned on the lights in the kitchen and the back porch light for Dad to see his way home, parted the blackout curtains, and began tidying the kitchen.

Hearing Dad's familiar whistle as he walked up the sidewalk put Betsy's heart at ease once again. Now she could concentrate on her homework – and outline a plan for the first "freedom for all" committee meeting.

CHAPTER 11

God Bless America

The bleachers were packed, some folks standing along the side-lines for a close look at the field, excitement for tonight's game against the Hodgeville Hawks fairly sizzled. Finding her place in the band's woodwind section, Betsy paused, simply wanting to set worries about Johnny aside and instead soak up all the flavors of her favorite season – the smell of leaves wrapping themselves in flames of orange, gold, and red; the sound of their crunching to each step she took; roasting wieners and marshmallows over the glow of a campfire; the bite of frost soon to come. And Friday night football games, marching with the band at half-time, dancing to music from the juke box in the crepe-paper decorated school gym afterwards – the fellows on the team stepping onto the floor fresh from the shower room dressed in cream-colored cord pants that stopped just above their saddle shoes, exchanging football strategies for dancing the steps to a waltz or the jitterbug. Smooth, quick, confident on the field, clumsy on the dance floor.

The pep club girls in their black skirts and sloppy Joe sweaters, a thick red letter "P" embroidered high on the left side, chattered among themselves in the section next to the band. Betsy, Ruthie, and Rosemary – all woodwinds – began arranging themselves, their instruments, and music books.

Ruthie startled them with a shrill whistle, let out her breath. "Gosh, every one of those fellows on their team is built like Li'l Abner! Compared to them, our lineup looks like Casper Milquetoasts."

Betsy stopped putting her saxophone together and looked. Her spirits sank. Both teams, Plainsview Warriors on one side of the fifty-yard line, Hawks from Hodgeville on the other – running a battery of calisthenics on the tired grass field – barking calls, doing pushups, sit ups, jumping jacks, drills. Shoulder pads cracked, helmets popped, cleats shot sprays of dirt and grass. Breaths puffed out in miniature clouds. You didn't have to be a genius to see what Ruthie meant about what they were up against.

Someone a few rows down grumbled, "Holy cow, we'll be lucky to get...."

"Size isn't everything," Colleen Sherman interrupted in a voice sharp as a butcher knife. "Don't forget. Blackie's the smartest and best quarterback in the state of Colorado."

"As if she'd ever let us forget," Rosemary muttered, clarinet across her lap.

"And look at that poor excuse for a pep club..." Colleen sneered, pointing to the small visitors' bleachers on the other side of the field where a lone cheerleader waved purple and white pompons, "...how can any team win without a cheering section?"

"Well, now, I wouldn't go that far," Ron said, beat a rat-a-tat-tat on his snare drum, winked at Colleen. "She's kinda cute, reminds me of June Allyson. Look at her yelling her lungs out and boy, can she do the splits."

"Humph." Colleen lifted her nose in the air.

Someone else announced, "If you ask me, they did a swell job getting enough gas for one carload to make that drive."

"Fat difference that'll make," Colleen shot back.

Betsy was tempted to blast a shrill "blllaaat!" on her sax right at Colleen's scarlet-painted lips.

"Forget about them," Ron piped up. "We're here for *our* team."

Just then squeals shrilled from the pep club section. Several girls stood up, clutching their skirts tight around them, and stared down. *"I see London, I see France...."* a chorus of boys' voices followed by crude laughter came from beneath the bleachers. Superintendent Sievers, patrolling back and forth and up and down the stands appeared, reached down, and nabbed a boy by the collar. Spud Sherman. Of course. Mr. Sievers ordered Spud and his buddies out. The girls sat down again, everyone in hearing distance watching to see what happened next.

The boys, looking cowed but defiant, crept out and stood in front of the superintendent.

"Up to more mischief, I see," Mr. Sievers said. Nobody, but nobody, could look directly into that angular face with the bushy brows pulled tight together beneath the frown, much less the pointed jaw and thin mouth turned down in permanent disapproval. "Picking on girls, playing with cigarettes and matches." He paused. "Pick up that package of Camels and box of matches and hand them over to me. Then go home."

"My father's president of the school board," Spud muttered, a sullen look on his face. "He can get you fired."

"Do as I said and no back talk." There was no mistaking the superintendent's tone.

Colleen stood up and peered through the bleachers close enough to say between clenched teeth, "Spencer Sherman, leave."

"You can't boss me. I'll tell on you. You know what."

Colleen would do anything to keep her parents from knowing she was crazy about some boy from the wrong side of town. It wouldn't matter to them that he was the best looking fellow in school, a great athlete, and made the Honor Roll, too. If they knew... they'd probably ship her out of town.

Rosemary edged closer to Betsy. "I wonder how Blackie's parents feel about him liking a girl on this side of town."

That thought hadn't occurred to Betsy, but now she wondered, too.

Colleen pursed her lips and turned away. The boys handed over the cigarettes and matches to Superintendent Sievers, stomped down the bleachers, and out the gate. Pep club girls and band members settled back in place.

Kathleen, student director who took over when Mr. Rogers coached, rapped her baton for attention. "Five minutes for warm up." The fellows in helmets and thin grass and mud-stained uniforms weren't the only ones who needed to warm up. A cacophony of brass, percussion, woodwinds filled the night until Kathleen rapped her baton again. Betsy opened her music book to *"The Star Spangled Banner."* She always had trouble hitting the high notes in that one even on the saxophone. She was glad she wasn't playing oboe tonight. That double reed had split a week ago and there was no knowing when Mr. Rogers could drive to Wells Music Store in Denver for instrument supplies like new reeds for saxes, clarinets, and her oboe.

"Holy smokes! What's going on?"

Betsy looked up at the percussion section. Red Cameron stood on tiptoe, neck craned, pointing his bass drum mallet.

Soon everyone in the stands turned to see, some on their feet, all straining their eyes. Two Army trucks had pulled in at the far end of the field and parked. U.S. soldiers jumped out, barked commands. Huddles of men dressed in the now familiar blue denim clothes marked "P.O.W." climbed out of the truck beds, formed a straight line facing the football field.

A buzz hummed from the crowd. Who invited them? They shouldn't be allowed outside that camp! What if...? No one had known this would be allowed. To be sure two truck beds of prisoners didn't equal the camp population, growing faster by the day, but still – why?

Ruthie leaned from the bleacher behind Betsy and Rosemary. "I wonder if they know what football is?"

Betsy didn't know what to think. A mix of emotions churned inside her – fear, disbelief, mixed with a little curiosity. Ruthie didn't seem worried. Just – interested.

"They've no right to be here." Colleen couldn't let this surprise go without a negative comment. "But now that they are, I intend to ignore them. I'm here to watch the game, not a freak show."

The novelty soon wore off and all eyes focused once again on the playing field. A big game to win. American soldiers stood guard over the prisoners.

A pair of solemn-faced Boy Scouts marched out to raise the flag and the crowd hushed, rose to their feet, hands on their hearts. Both teams stood at attention, helmets off. School Superintendent Sievers led the pledge of allegiance... the final words "with liberty and justice for all" echoing again in Betsy's ears. "Justice for all." That's why "our boys" were fighting. And those words had given her the courage to do something about righting a wrong, even if it was a small something. When Johnny did come home, she hoped he'd be proud of her.

Kathleen raised her baton and the band blared the melody of *"The Star Spangled Banner"* as the crowd joined in singing, some voices true and loud, others off-key, some a note behind, but each one exuberant.

The teams faced each other in formation at the fifty-yard line, the crowd was on their feet cheering, clapping, whistling, and stomping – then collectively held their breaths for the kickoff by the home team. The ball sailed high and far straight into the Hawk receiver's hands. Like a shot out of a cannon, he hurtled down the field, made mincemeat of every defensive Warrior trying for a tackle, crossed the goal line and lifted the ball in the air. Their kicker made the extra point and within the first minutes of the quarter the score was Hawks – 7, Warriors – 0.

The lone visiting cheerleader and handful of fans cheered their loudest, stamped, whistled, clapped, threw their arms in the air. The sound in the home bleachers resembled something like air slowly releasing from a big balloon. Kathleen signaled the band to play Hodgeville High's school song and the cheerleaders called a spirited cheer, the home team folks giving a token response.

Then they switched to cheers for Plainsville High, "Go, Warriors, go – fight – win!" The band turned up the volume for the school song, the crowd standing and singing, clapping the rhythm. The autumn air turned magically electric.

And then what sounded like an echo from the end of the field came the sound of men's voices, "Go, Varriors, go…go Varriors…vin!"

Heads swiveled, people gawked. Two war prisoners stood in front of the others, imitating the cheerleaders *(minus the splits and somersaults)* and leading the other men. They clapped and shouted. Cynthia, senior cheerleader, didn't waste a minute, but directed the hometown fans to join in. Not once but *three* times.

Ruthie and Betsy grabbed hands, looked at each other, in sheer amazement.

Now their team had the ball and Blackie strong-armed a pass. A tall, bulky Hawk pulled the pass out of the air, turned, and headed for his goal post, cradling the ball. The Warriors were ready, though, and a half dozen of them tackled him. The ball popped loose and – a Warrior moved in to grab it and race toward the home team's goal. There was no mistaking who that player was – tall, skinny, all elbows and knees Jack Gordon, the player Colleen claimed shouldn't be allowed to be the water boy. . . . In the confusion that followed, Jack – the ball tucked tight in his arm – had sped down the length of the field and crossed the goal line. Ruthie tapped Colleen on the shoulder. "Guess who just put the Warriors on the scoreboard, Colleen, and it wasn't Blackie."

"Luck. Pure luck," Colleen snapped back. "Just wait and you'll see who's the bright star of this game."

Another round of the Warriors song, cheerleaders cart-wheeling, doing flips – bolstered by the P.O.W.s chanting, "Go, Varriors, go, fight, vin!" The prisoners seemed to be having a good time, Betsy thought. For some reason, she dared to hope that Johnny would soon be found. Unharmed.

After those high-pitched opening moments, the game settled in, the Hawks soon pulling ahead to win by a wide margin. The Warriors had made a mighty effort and gotten on the scoreboard with a total of 14 points – first touchdown by Jack, the second by Blackie.

According to custom in these war years, reverence filled the air as the crowd stood to sing *"God Bless America."* Always, those last four words. . ."my home sweet home". . . floated through the night sky toward the stars.

CHAPTER 12

Give It Your Best!

E ver since the class meeting, Willie had plunged head first into the "Justice for All" project. Colleen and her crowd could object till they were blue in the face, and Willie didn't give a hoot. Maybe playing the class clown could be an advantage, Betsy thought – he could dare to be different. And maybe, too, the fact that he stood up for what he believed in made the others really pay attention. The majority voted to approve taking on the project. Only a few were dead set against it. Was it *fear* that closed their minds – fear of what? Or was it something else? Betsy was beginning to realize that not everyone saw the world the way she did.

When the committee of five held their first meeting, Willie volunteered to co-chair the project with Betsy. Betsy's mind went into a spin. Co-chair a project like this with Willie – the boy whose antics seemed so childish, so crazy, so pointless? Had a serious thought ever entered his head? She didn't know what to think and looked at their class sponsor, hoping she'd say something. Anything. Mrs. Frei said nothing, her arms folded across her chest, her face a mask.

This was her idea, Betsy reminded herself, but how was she to know what to do? And they needed to get started, maybe by asking shop owners to remove the "whites only" signs but there had to be more, too. The school break for harvest was coming soon. So she settled for simply thanking Willie and called for ideas.

Glenn went first. "We could make a list of things we want to accomplish, then divide into teams," he suggested. "Assign teams different businesses so we don't bombard them."

"And tell people why it's important," Willie added. "What you said, Betsy, about 'freedom and justice for all,' not just for those who 'talk American' and whose skin is the right color."

Willie really is serious about this, Betsy thought.

Rosemary pushed her glasses up on her nose. "What do we say to grownups who'll think we're just a bunch of teenagers stirring up trouble. The people who want things left as they are."

"Like Mr. Slipher for one," Leland said. "Who gets to walk into his office? Draw straws?" He didn't try to hide his sarcasm.

A chorus of groans responded.

Rosemary came up with another thought. "I think we should talk to all the business owners, not just the ones with 'whites only' signs," she said. "People need to know the facts. Otherwise the gossip will get out of hand."

"The gossips will have their fun no matter what." Glenn shook his head, seeming resigned to the fact. Then he went on, "Rosie's right. We don't want people to think we're going behind their backs."

"All in favor?" Betsy asked, adding Rosie's suggestion to the list.

"What about clubs? Schools? Especially civics classes."

"Or should we take it one step at a time, see what response we get before we wade in too deep?"

The ideas flowed, a plan was devised, and the proposal presented at the next class meeting. After discussion on both sides of the issue, Chuck – as class president – called for the vote. The motion passed: 29 for, 7 against. The bell rang ending lunch hour and Colleen and her followers clambered out of their desks, muttering remarks like "... tell those Mexicans to keep their place..." and "... stir up a bunch of trouble...."

Mrs. Frei marshaled students out the door. "This discussion is over," she announced in that familiar don't-argue-with-me tone. "From here on every sophomore is to accept and honor that choice. I don't want to hear anything negative. Not here, not outside the school doors."

~

Now on this sky blue Saturday morning, Betsy and Willie met in front of the Honor Roll board on Main Street, their list of business owners in hand. Fred Hopper called and waved from the top step of the ladder where he was starting a new column of names.

"You two are looking mighty serious on a no-school day. I trust you're not up to any mischief," he said, eyes twinkling.

Willie told him about their project – and added that he and Betsy were deciding whether to make Mr. Slipher their first visit and get it over with or put his name last on their list.

"Whew-ee!" Fred whistled, took off his cap, and scratched his head, leaving fingerprints of blue paint. "You've got a pretty big mission here. I hope the *Sun* is writing it up for this week's edition."

"Well, not quite the *Sun*, at least not yet," Betsy said. "But our school paper for sure." She'd been assigned to type up that article for the first quarter's mimeographed issue. There wasn't enough paper to put their news out more often, and she hoped their sponsor, Miss Price, would bury this piece on an inside page. She was already feeling too self-conscious.

"We figure we'd better start small," Willie said. His gaze went from Fred to the freshly painted name on the Honor Roll board. And to the gold star added in front of Donald Davis's name, but none of the three said a word, each thinking their own thoughts.

Fred frowned and nodded. "My vote says it's the best home front project yet," he said. "After all, there has to be a reason for the sacrifices war demands."

Betsy watched him glance at the gold star, then away again.

"Nothing like fighting a battle without guns," Willie quipped, making one of his famous cross-eyed, dumb ox faces.

Fred gave them the "V" for victory sign and dipped his brush in the paint. "Give it your best!" he called after them, "Like the poster says."

"Double that when we knock on Mr. Slipher's door," Betsy answered back. Her stomach knotted.

"Hey, Betsy, you're not gonna let that oily-haired, so-called big shot scare you, are you?" Willie turned to squint at her.

Betsy braced herself. "Well, I have to admit I get the creeps just looking at him. What could anyone possibly say that he'd actually hear?"

"He's not exactly the approachable type, for sure," Willie said between gritted teeth. "Just don't let on to him that you're nervous. Act with conviction."

"Right," Betsy said. "Let's knock on his door first, see the others on our list, and save Clyde Willowby's barber shop for dessert."

Willie touched Betsy's shoulder, paused. "Look, Betsy, let's face facts." When her eyebrows raised in an unspoken question, he explained. "Don't think I'm running out on you, but the truth is he's never gonna take me seriously. I mean, nobody does, really. And he's kicked me out of the theatre right in the middle of the main feature more times than I can count. He and his flashlight announcing to the whole world who's been rowdy. At least his definition of that word. That old grouch has got it in for me."

"But, Willie," Betsy said, turning to face him, "you promised. You can't send me in there alone."

"I'll be waiting for you right here. What I'm saying is that first we need to get in the door. If you're the one who knocks, he'll at least let you come inside."

Now Betsy's stomach was churning louder than Mom's washing machine under a load of rag rugs. "You're not the only one he doesn't take seriously. He's always calling me things like 'girlie' and scolding me for not getting Mrs. Slipher's groceries to her on time."

Willie squared his jaw.

"Look. Just walk in there, sit in the chair across from his desk, and tell him about it the same way you told our class. Convince him of the importance of our goal, maybe tell him to think it over a few days before giving his answer. Who cares what he says?"

Willie planted himself at the outside door, gave Betsy a nudge and the victory sign. She took three deep breaths, walked through the lobby to the door labeled "Harvey P. Slipher – Owner and Manager," and knocked.

CHAPTER 13

We Can – We Must – We Will Do It!

Sure, the work would be hard, they'd told themselves. Four "town girls" – Betsy, Emily, Fran, and Mary Beth – who had happy memories of visiting a friend's farm, gathering eggs from hens' nests, wading in the irrigation ditch, swinging in the big rubber truck tire that hung on a fat rope from a sturdy branch of the cottonwood tree, feasting on fried chicken and mashed potatoes for lunch. What they hadn't seen was the work of it. When they learned the true meaning of hard that first day, they never wanted to come back. To hold tight to their resolve, they kept that poster image of Rosie the Riveter in front of their minds, a cute, red-lipsticked Rosie flexing her muscles and proclaiming "We Can Do It." Remembering the poster girl's motto plus reminding themselves that every potato they tossed in a burlap bag helped feed the troops – as the slogan said, "Food Wins War."

The sun hadn't yet risen when Mr. Fritzler stopped to collect them at Betsy's house on the corner of Main and Walnut Streets that first Monday after school closed for harvest. Straw hats, work gloves, and brown bag lunches in hand, they'd squeezed in next to him on the wide front seat of his truck. His farm was three miles northeast of town and the potato field assigned to the girls lay just beyond the bright red barn.

They'd wrapped their heads in Aunt Jemima bandanas *(red with white polka dots like Rosie's, but – like Aunt Jemima – they didn't come close to looking pretty and perky like Rosie)* under wide straw hats to shield their hair against sweat and dirt, their faces against the relentless rays of the sun as the morning wore on. They wore their dads' worn, long-sleeved shirts, their oldest pairs of blue jeans, thrice-darned socks, old shoes, and men's work gloves. Armed and ready for the battle of the potatoes. That's what they'd thought before dawn on Monday.

Mr. Fritzler led the way to the frost-blanketed field where rows of freshly plowed potatoes lay scattered, gave them brief instructions, and left. Betsy and Emily dropped to their knees, one on each side of a row; the next row down Fran and Mary Beth did the same – each girl equipped with a big bucket. When they filled a bucket, they dumped the potatoes into a scratchy burlap bag – 50 pounds? 100? When a gunnysack was full, they left it standing in the field. Later a farm hand would load the bags onto the truck and haul them away for shipping. During the early morning hours, the clods of plowed earth were hard as bricks – their unforgiving ridges cutting into their knees. Hands, too. Before mid-morning the clods softened but were difficult to maneuver. By then they'd shed their jackets and tied them around their waists. Crawling all day on hands and knees over jagged clods of dirt brought them to their knees in more ways than one. Betsy thought about their girlfriends from the other side of town who'd grown up stooping all day to thin the plants, hoeing to cultivate and weed, and finally topping sugar beets just like the older boys and grown men. They resolved to toughen up and made a game of the work, calling out with each potato they tossed in a bucket, "Bombs over Tokyo" – or Berlin or Rome, Hitler, Mussolini, Hiro Hito. They sang at the top of their lungs – the Marine song, the Air Force – Army – Navy and then the popular tunes like *"Don't Sit Under the Apple Tree"* and *"This Is the Army Mr. Jones," "Wait for Me, Mary,"* and *"When the Lights Come On Again."* And then they'd be quiet for a while, each girl lost in her own thoughts. They paused now and then to drink water out of Mason jars their mothers had sent with them.

A couple of times, at the rare sound of an airplane – a B-17 or B-29 – they stopped work to sit back on their knees, shield their eyes against the glare of the sun, and look to the sky, following the plane's path as it flew toward Lowry Air Base in Denver. Maybe they'd get lucky and see the propellers turning or catch a glimpse inside the cockpit and see the pilot wearing his black leather aviator helmet.

By afternoon the mood swung to goofy. They giggled over

anything and nothing, little moron jokes, the way they looked – dirt-smudged ragamuffins. How many times did they repeat the riddle "What does Hitler say when a new baby's born? – Hotsy totsy, another little Nazi," then toss a potato into the bucket to bomb those Nazis. They squealed when a field mouse scampered across, skinny tail trailing behind it. They paused now and then to wipe sweat from their flushed faces with their sleeves and shirttails. When they'd finally poured the last buckets of potatoes into gunny sacks, the skin on their knees was scraped and bleeding, bones and muscles they didn't know they had were screaming, sweat and dirt drenched their clothes. They'd worked from freezing in the morning to stifling heat at noon, and now with the sun beginning its slide behind the mountain peaks a softer warmth carried on a breeze.

At noon they'd taken their lunches to the shade of a grove of cottonwood trees along the irrigation ditch. Horseflies hovered over their sandwiches, giant horseflies that plunged poison stingers straight through their thin cotton shirts seeking out tender flesh. The girls had never been so hungry, never so stiff and sore. When they stretched out in the shade to eat and talk and then lie down with their straw hats over their faces, it felt like heaven.

They gossiped about the latest "crush" some girlfriend had, catalogued complaints about teachers and shopkeepers – especially Mr. Slipher, who had refused to remove the arrow pointing to the balcony at the movie theatre, the designated seating for people of darker skin color. They congratulated themselves for having organized a boycott on the Saturday night movie. Not a single ticket was sold that night, not even to grownups, and Mr. Slipher fumed and spewed and phoned the next day to scold the superintendent of schools.

They chortled over that. Fran repeated the rest of that story. "Willie says if one of the theatre ushers allows a Mexican to sit on the main floor, sign or no sign, he'll get fired."

"Yeah. And those ushers need the work. So who won that battle?"

"Maybe we both did," Emily said, her forehead furrowed with thought. "Remember what Clyde Willowby at the barbershop cautioned us."

"That we can't change the whole world overnight," Mary Beth chimed in, fanning a horsefly away with her straw hat.

Betsy finished that statement: "But maybe we can change it one step at a time. And we did take that first step."

That was lunchtime. They'd made it halfway through the day.

Now at day's end they looked more like war orphans than "Rosie the Riveter." They collected their belongings, waited for Mr. Fritzler, looked at each other and announced, "We did it!"

They piled back into Mr. Fritzler's Ford truck. "Not bad for your first day," he said, smiling, and they were off in a cloud of dust on the country road back to town.

"Betsy, you're home!" Billie called, racing to meet the truck at the curb. He jumped into her arms and, exhausted as she was, she lifted him up and swung him 'round and 'round.

Cat was right behind him, talking a mile a minute. "Guess how many deliveries I made today, Big Sis – eight altogether, five this morning and three this afternoon and lemonade and cookies at Mrs. Newsom's kitchen table. And a scolding from Mrs. Slipher for being five minutes late. Oh, and guess what? Helen got a letter from Hal at the army hospital." A month or so ago Helen had been almost relieved when she got the telegram saying Hal had been wounded in action. Relieved to know that he was back in the States. He was alive. He wasn't on a battlefield across the ocean. Now letters arrived from the hospital daily, wanting to know about her and the children, telling how he was learning to walk with a wooden leg. Still, Betsy thought, German soldiers and done that to Hal. Germans. Like the ones at the prison camp here.

Betsy, Cat, and Billie sat right down on the grass that was still summer soft and green and wearing a mix of gold, orange, and yellow-green leaves. Betsy hugged them both. How good it was to be home. Then they stood to go in through the kitchen door – Billie carrying her empty brown bag and water jug, Cat taking her work gloves, hat, and bandana. Betsy left her shoes and dirty jeans and shirt on the back porch, wrapping herself in an old chenille robe hanging there on a hook.

Mom looked up from paring apples for a Waldorf salad, shook her head. "Oh, Betsy, just look at those raw knees of yours!" she said and promised to sew thick knee pads to her jeans tonight, shooed her into the bathroom for a sink bath. No bath in the tub till Saturday night as usual, but shedding her muddy clothes and scrubbing all over with hot soapy water was the best feeling ever. The smell of a casserole in the oven set Betsy's mouth watering. Tired as she was, she was hungry enough to devour her supper and everyone else's, too. Dad glanced up from the evening edition of *The Denver Post* and gave her that little grin of his that went along with the familiar twinkle in his blue eyes. He looked fresh from a long afternoon nap and clean work clothes, ready for his graveyard shift – midnight to 8 a.m. – at the factory.

As for Betsy, a hot supper, a soothing rubdown from Mom, and the cozy warmth of flannel pajamas was a recipe for falling asleep the minute her head hit the pillow.

And crawled along clod-ridden rows of potatoes in her sleep.

CHAPTER 14

Praise the Lord and Pass the Ammunition

"Ooooo–ick!" Betsy sank back on her heels in the dirt, pulled off the soaked glove.

Emily pinched her nostrils shut. "Not another rotten potato," Emily moaned, casting a look at Betsy as if it were her fault. "Phew-ee. Smells bad enough to poison the enemy, if you ask me."

"Here's a riddle for you – Which is slimier and stinkier – ," Fran called from the next row, "a rotten potato or Mr. Slipher?" A chorus of groans answered. Fran and Mary Beth scrambled several yards ahead of them, tossing potatoes into their buckets with frenzy.

The sun was high in the sky now, its heat intensifying the foul odor. Betsy was doomed to wear that glove, soaked through with that horrid smell, the rest of the day. And she thought she'd been so careful to watch for any rotting ones. Why hadn't she brought along Dad's worn work gloves as a spare pair the way Mom suggested? She rubbed the glove in dirt, hoping to smother the smell.

They worked awhile without talking. Then Mary Beth stopped. "Time for a water break," she announced. They allowed themselves several sips, careful to ration the remainder. It had to last the rest of the day. Once in a while, Mrs. Fritzler sent ten-year-old Frankie out with a pitcher of lemonade for them in the middle of the afternoon. Cold lemonade never tasted so good.

"Not long now before we finish this field," Emily announced, a note of satisfaction in her voice. "By that time, we ought to qualify as professional field hands."

"Well, maybe not 'professional,'" Fran said, "but definitely 'experienced.' We've got the ragged remains of blue jeans and shirts as evidence." They looked at each other and shook their heads. "We've even developed some biceps in the process, the only part of us faintly resembling 'Rosie the Riveter.'" As if on cue they grinned, showed off their new muscles, then made the victory sign.

They'd worked their way closer to the end of the field when Mary Beth's breath caught loud enough to get all their attention. She motioned toward the irrigation ditch. "Golly, those Germans are getting way too close for comfort." The prisoners in the sugar beet field on the other side of the irrigation ditch had worked their way toward the potato field.

"Don't look," Emily said. "I don't want them staring at us."

"Oh, pooh!" Fran scoffed. "They're topping beets so fast they don't have time to look up. Besides, the guards are watching. And they've got guns."

Betsy noted the pair of soldiers resting in the shade of a cottonwood. "Doesn't look like they're paying that much attention."

The girls kept working their way down the long rows of now not-so-freshly-dug potatoes. Even the clods of dirt felt almost hot enough to blister their hands. What would they do without heavy work gloves?

"I've heard they don't take any mean prisoners outside the camp gates. So the ones we're seeing are here to get Mr. Fritzler's beets topped. I don't think they'll get out of line," Emily pointed out. "And we already know that without them a lot of the beets would be left to rot." She shook her head and added, "But I have to admit I can't help feeling scared. The enemy within yards of us armed with wicked-looking knives."

Mary Beth shook her head. "War sure is strange." There was a long pause when she said that, each of them turning this strangeness in their thoughts.

"We'd better get on with our own job and not let them slow us down." Betsy bent down and doubled her potato picking speed. At least for now.

Changing the subject, Betsy mused, "When we get paid, I'll have enough savings stamps to fill my book for a $25 bond. And 'bonds buy bombs,' which means our work is doing double duty. Isn't that swell?"

"And after the war's over," Emily said, "we can cash the bonds to help pay for college. Otherwise, most of our folks can't afford to send us. More than one reason to stick with this job."

Fran and Mary Beth were a few yards ahead of Emily and Betsy but heard what they'd said. "Maybe I'm not being patriotic enough, but just between us I'm keeping some of my money in a separate envelope," Fran confessed. "I want something brand new for the Homecoming Dance, an outfit that Grandma hasn't made from Grandpa's old three-piece, gray pin-striped suit."

"Remember when we were little how a lot of girls' mothers sewed dresses out of those printed flour sacks? Some kids turned up their noses at a flour sack dress, but there really were some pretty ones."

"How much longer is this war going to go on?" Mary Beth's shoulders sagged as she tossed two more potatoes into her bucket. "Sometimes this business of 'making do with less' gets kind of old."

"I clipped out an ad from this month's issue of *Calling All Girls,*" Betsy told them. "It's for a cute jumper embroidered with tiny flowers around the neckline and it comes in my favorite color – aqua. I'm so tempted to send off for it even if it does cost almost ten dollars."

"Oh, Betsy," Fran urged, "send for it. It has to be okay to reward ourselves every once in awhile."

Mary Beth chimed in. "After all, we have to keep our spirits up, too."

"Besides, from what I hear," Emily added, "some of our servicemen, including my brother, Ed, will be home on leave for Homecoming. We need new outfits to welcome them."

Betsy studied her filthy clothes, the glove now stiff from the rotten potato. Maybe she would send for the jumper.

The sun told them it was okay to stop for lunch soon, though they'd been hungry for more than two hours. When they got to the end of the rows they were picking, they set down their buckets and hurried into the shade of the trees, relieved to peel off their gloves, hats and bandanas, and shoes for a half hour or so. As usual, there was a bit of trading and sharing of the lunches their mothers had packed – sandwiches wrapped in waxed paper, Jonathan apples, a few treats tucked in. Each girl had two whole sandwiches, cut into halves. Fran swapped one of her mother's home baked dark bread sandwiches with Betsy for a Spamwich between slices of white Rainbow bread. Mary Beth shared a small jar of her mother's canned apricots and Betsy a jar of Grandma Blakesly's bread and butter pickles. Emily divided a Hershey's milk chocolate candy bar among them and they pooled their carrot and celery sticks.

In the sugar beet field, the prisoners and their two guards had stopped to eat lunch, too. A few of them gnawed on slices cut from a sugar beet. Not long ago the town grapevine complained that the prisoners got more food than local people do. After that the prisoners' rations got cut. Maybe a little too much if the ones doing farm work didn't get enough to eat. The girls couldn't help looking at them now and then and wondering about what kinds of food they were fed – American food? Or German – like the Germans from Russia on farms here or in Mill Town. And how did they think about prisoners at the camp who didn't work in the fields but stayed inside the camp – like officers, for example, and a small group of Nazis so loyal to Hitler they had to be kept separate from the others.

Mary Beth chewed on a carrot stick. Then, brightening, changed the subject. "So who do you think will be Homecoming Queen?"

"Joyce Adkins gets my vote. She's so cute with that soft, wavy blonde hair and big brown eyes and besides that she's nice to everyone."

"Whoever the queen is, she has to be a senior. And Blackie Hoffman's a sure bet for King. I can almost see Colleen Sherman turning green with jealousy watching a girl like Joyce sitting next to Blackie on matching thrones."

"If you want my opinion, Colleen will be lucky to be the sophomore attendant. Even if she is the prettiest girl in our class."

"We'd better get back to work," Emily announced. Reluctantly, they folded the sheets of waxed paper, collected their spoons and jars, tucked them back in their brown bags, and tackled the next two rows of potatoes.

A couple of hours into the heat of that October afternoon they heard a sharp cry of pain coming from the beet field. A blue-denim clad worker stood jumping from foot to foot, the good hand gripping the blood-soaked one. The guards ordered the other prisoners to keep topping beets. The taller guard rushed over, pulled off both his outer and under shirts. Ripping the white cotton undershirt apart, he tied on a tourniquet. Next he lifted his canteen of water to the prisoner's lips, then began walking the man, arm clutched tight against his shirt, toward the farmhouse.

For once the four girls sat in the dirt speechless. At last Betsy breathed, "No wonder my dad won't let me top beets."

There was nothing to do but get back to work again, so the four-some began where they'd left off. They'd barely begun when Emily looked across at Betsy. "Gee, kid," she said, "I'm about to wet my pants. Gotta run for the weeds."

Betsy watched her disappear among the weeds growing along the irrigation ditch. Betsy wasn't sure how long she could wait before following Em. She guessed that Fran and Mary Beth would be next. They'd all been that scared. But they'd have to work fast to make up for lost time. The time of day when their bodies were almost too worn out to move.

A scream pierced from the weeds. Em. Muttering in German, a prisoner stood a few feet from her. The lone guard swiveled his head, aimed his rifle, shouted, "Halt!" But the prisoner didn't halt. Instead he turned and ran, a shot rang out but the prisoner kept running. The soldier on guard called to the girls, "You're not in danger. Best you get back to your potatoes."

Em half ran, half strode toward them, her face showing chalk white beneath the layer of dirt and sunburn. She sighed with relief as she reached the others but couldn't stop shaking. "I thought he was coming after me," she said. "He had this awful look in his eyes and kept talking German. German!"

"How did he get away from the guard?" Fran wanted to know.

"And why?" Betsy asked, her arm tight around Em's shoulder.

Mary Beth shrugged. "How should we know? But here, Em, you need to take a big drink of water and just lie down in the dirt for a few minutes."

First a bleeding prisoner, then a runaway one. They all needed time to calm down. And maybe, Betsy thought, for once they'd be glad to get down on hands and knees again, helping to feed American troops.

Overhead the sound of a B-29 bomber turned their faces skyward. There was the comforting sight of an airplane on its way to the air base in Denver. And always a plane made her think of her cousin Johnny.

"Look," Mary Beth squealed, "there's the pilot!"

The plane dipped low, the pilot saluted. Gasping surprise, the girls returned his salute, then watched the plane out of sight against the backdrop of the mountains.

They looked at one another, wide-eyed. "Imagine that," Emily breathed. Betsy sang out, *"Praise the Lord and pass the ammunition!"*

CHAPTER 15

United?

F or the second time now Mrs. Newsom was sending Betsy and Jack out to the prison camp with a care package. A few days after the double shock of that afternoon in the potato field, Doc Wendling had been called to the prison camp's infirmary to assist in caring for both the wounded men – the injuries from the beet knife for one and for the gun shot wound the other. Then he'd appealed to Mrs. Newsom's care package committee. Once again Doc Wendling and the trio of women shrugged off complaints from some of the townspeople. Both injured prisoners were young – no more than 16 years old, Doc said, and homesick.

Betsy wasn't sure how she felt. For one thing, that prisoner who'd gotten so close to Em had scared the wits out of her. Had he intended to hurt her? What had he planned to do? How could anyone be sure about either of those prisoners? After all, they were Germans – the enemy – and it was a German who'd shot down her cousin Johnny.

The other side of her asked: Shouldn't we treat these men the way we'd want the enemy to treat captured Americans? If Johnny were in one of their camps right now, were they giving him enough to eat? Warm clothes? Medical treatment if he needed it?

Not everyone in Plainsview agreed with Doc Wendling's philosophy and said so in hearing range of everyone waiting for mail in the post office. Every single one of those 3,000 prisoners was an enemy, they argued, Hitler's henchmen, waiting to jump at the chance to harm us.

Mrs. Newsom shooed them out to the car, Jack carrying the pan of cinnamon rolls. Betsy asked him to set the rolls on the seat between them. He hurried to the driver's side and settled in, glanced across and teased, "Are you sure you can't move any closer to the door,

Betsy B.? I might bite, you know." He bared his teeth.

Betsy looked away, made sure the door was locked, and leaned against it.

Mrs. Newsom, along with Mrs. Taylor and Mrs. Sundstrom, smiled and waved as Jack eased the clutch out and shifted into first, his right foot pressing the gas pedal. His father's black Chevy sedan was clean and polished, like always. Jack was known to spend an entire Saturday or Sunday afternoon washing and waxing, pulling out the seats to whisk away dirt and debris. Maybe that's why Mr. Gordon didn't put up much of an argument when Jack wanted to use it. Like today. Besides, Jack's dad agreed with Doc about the boys who needed some home baking. They were boys, after all – boys doing men's fighting.

As he turned onto the road to Greeley, Jack asked, "Is it true that you and your potato partners saw that accident happen? And the other fellow run off?"

Betsy nodded. "The accident – what we could see from across the irrigation ditch, a few rows of potatoes and some of beets. Then the runaway – almost face to face with Em! Scared us all to death."

Jack nodded. "Those topping knives. Dangerous work. Hard work, and heavy. Even for men who've grown up doing it. This fellow might have been a city kid. Wouldn't know a sugar beet from a potato."

Betsy pictured how those fields had grown over the summer months – the rich earth plowed, smoothed, and planted in straight rows in early spring, the young sugar beet plants hoed and thinned twice by hired hands – mostly girls and women from Mill Town or living in a small house on a farm owner's land – the mature plants' big, dark green leaves spreading across the ground, irrigation water flowing along ditches next to the plants, monster-size beets developing unseen beneath the surface.

Potatoes, too, grew beneath the ground – each plant spreading more delicately and taller than the sugar beet plants – and covered with white blossoms in late summer, a sure sign the potatoes were forming in the earth – lots of them to each plant. Just one big beet (five or more pounds) to each plant – a person could eat potatoes raw or cooked a half dozen ways or more; not so, the sugar beet. . .

those had to go for processing into sugar at the factory. For Betsy as a first time worker, starting down each row to pick the freshly plowed potatoes, the task seemed endless. She couldn't imagine how it must feel to start down a row of beets, a task more complicated, heavy, and demanding. And for that young prisoner – she sighed.

"That memory chasing through your head, is it, Betsy?" Jack's tone softened, not like his usual, teasing banter.

She glanced at him, nodded. "Not the first time, either, but I wish it could be the last."

"Well, that prisoner's not the only person whose knife has slipped. Experienced worker or not, accidents do happen. As for the runaway, who knows why he did a crazy thing like that?"

"Yes, why. That's what feels like a dark shadow to me."

"We'll probably never know. But now for us, timeout from school is over. It's back to pencils and notebooks, homework and tests." He paused and added, "and scrap collecting, bond drives, the last of the football season, and Homecoming."

The car rounded that familiar bend in the road where the landscape changed briefly from flat and open fields to a gently rolling, wooded little meadow. The place where the abandoned farmhouse and sagging barn, all the paint worn off, sat looking lonely and uncared for.

Betsy sat up straighter and leaned forward. "Jack, look," she said, "isn't that Mr. Slipher's car parked over there between the barn and the house? What would he be doing here?"

Jack squinted. "His big Buick without a doubt. And another car in the shadows . . . looks like a Denver license plate. Maybe he's thinking of buying that property cheap and selling it after the war for a big profit."

"Mmmmm . . . maybe. But it sure seems strange."

By then they'd rounded the curve and driven up the hill toward the camp. Hatless, his jacket, shirt, and tie loosened, Sergeant Bill Hoff waited at the gate, stepped through to clamp Jack's shoulder and take the pan of rolls. Betsy glanced along the fence, relieved to see the watchdogs farther away. Bill apologized for his informality, saying, "October days sure can get hot," he said, "and these uniforms are – sweltering."

"You probably won't be marching in any parades this evening," Jack quipped.

"So good to see you two again," Bill said, his voice warm with pleasure. He paused to inhale the aroma of home baking.

"The poor kid messed himself up pretty bad. Kind of ironic... no war medals for wounds suffered here, serious or not. The one who tried to run off? Who knows?"

He turned to Betsy. "What's this I hear about a sophomore class project?"

Betsy stammered, felt her face flush. Why couldn't she be at ease with fellows, especially those a few years older, like Emily and Fran were? They never got flustered and seemed to know just the right responses.

"Betsy's not one to 'toot her own horn,' Bill," Jack answered for her, "but she did come up with a great class project – a way to take a step or two in making sure we uphold our country's values even though some people, whoever they are, aren't paying attention. Just wish I were a sophomore on that project."

Betsy spoke up. "You don't have to be a sophomore to join the effort, Jack. We want everyone who's willing to be involved."

"What a boost to the morale of those of us in uniform, Betsy," Bill said when Jack explained about the signs like *"whites only," "talk American,"* and *"Mexicans – seating in balcony only"* the committee members had persuaded business people to remove. The problem wasn't that big here, but the prejudice sure was.

"Good for you," Bill looked at Betsy. "Words like 'freedom' and 'justice for all' sound good, but they're just words if we don't live up to their meaning. And I'll bet some folks in town are fighting your group's efforts." Bill, being from a Mill Town family, could write his own story about prejudice.

All at once those scenes came up in her head again – the day she'd dropped her world history book and the note that fell out, a tightly folded scrap of tablet paper, another the next day in her Latin book, a third in the geometry text; and then she'd found another shoved through her locker door. The childlike printing, uneven lines, capitols in the wrong places, each letter a different color crayon said "Keep your nose out of our business!" At the end a skull and crossbones drawn in black followed by a splash of red. She'd turned ice cold. Felt a shadow hovering in the background, tried to guess whose shadow it was.

As if a dam had burst, a river of words spilled. "I've gotten hate notes between the pages of textbooks, inside my locker... sometimes it almost seems the whole town's against me."

Jack looked at her. "I didn't know you'd gotten threats, Betsy! Who did this? I don't suppose the cowards signed their names."

"Well, it's not something I wanted to broadcast. And I don't know why I told you now. I haven't told anyone else. I didn't know what to do, and I don't want my family to find out. They've got enough to worry about. All I wanted to do was try to right what seems to me to be a wrong, and instead I've started a war right here in Plainsview. And remember that poster – 'United We Stand'? Now I'm guilty of dividing us."

Bill laid his hand on her shoulder. "Betsy, what you're doing is right. It's what this war is about. I expect you stumbled across a few rotten potatoes in Mr. Fritzler's field. Well, there are always a few rotten potatoes among a whole crop of good, nutritious ones. That goes for people, too."

"Bill's right, Betsy. You have to believe in yourself and not let those rotten folks in our midst put an end to your effort."

Emotions boiled over inside her. She swallowed hard, looked at Bill and Jack. "Thanks. I'm glad I told you. I feel better now. And more determined, too."

"Atta girl," Bill said.

"Go get 'em." Jack winked and made the victory sign.

"Okay," Betsy said, "but promise you won't tell another soul about those threats. Promise, okay?"

The three shook hands. Betsy's chin lifted and she managed to put a smile on her face.

CHAPTER 16

String of Pearls

"Betsy!"

Arms loaded with grocery bags, Betsy turned at the familiar voice. "Hi, Willie! You doing errands for your mom, too?" She set her bags in the basket of her bike, ready to pedal home. There was a chill in the air today, maybe even a hint of snow. People walked up and down Main Street, leaving the post office with this morning's mail delivery, going in and out of the Five and Dime, Manweiler's Hardware, the *Plainsview Sun* with this week's edition of the news, Clyde's Barbershop, Ma Bell telephone office, Schmidt's Shoe Repair.

Willie crossed the street. "Could you take a few minutes to have a Coke with me?"

Betsy hesitated. What was Willie up to? "Well, I...."

"Look, it's not like a date or something. It's...."

For once he seemed at a loss for words. He wasn't grinning that crazy grin of his. In fact he wasn't grinning at all but wore a serious – even sober – look, Betsy thought.

Then, true to form, he crossed his eyes and traced circles next to his ear with an index finger – like the crazy kid everyone knew, then straightened up. "... well, it's about... it's kind of related to our class project." He fidgeted from one foot to the other. "You could maybe call it a sort of committee meeting. Of two."

"Well, sure, Willie, but... I mustn't stay long or Mom'll be wondering where her groceries are." She felt self-conscious. She'd never gone for a Coke with just one boy before. She'd always been part of a group – a group of girlfriends going in, a bunch of fellas hanging over the back of the next booth, everyone laughing and talking at once and staying way longer than they should. Yet there was something about Willie's manner – something that said he wasn't joking, wasn't flirting.

"We'll sit in that booth at the back. There won't be any other kids from school here this time of day." He grinned, the freckles on his face seeming to dance, and she relaxed a little.

Willie carried Betsy's grocery bags to the back booth, set them to the side of the red upholstered seat, helped Betsy take off her jacket and seated her. "Coast is clear," he said, glancing at the few grownups in the store. "What flavor will it be – cherry, chocolate, lemon? It's on me."

"I like chocolate," she said, "but you don't need to pay for it." She handed him a dime.

"Hey, this wasn't your idea." He pushed the dime back. "And this is about me asking for a favor. The least I can do is buy your Coke." He was off to the soda fountain. The drugstore had war posters on the walls like the post office and other places around town. But everyone knew Pete Taylor was a huge fan of Glenn Miller. Knew him personally. Met him at the University in Boulder where Miller had formed his own band there before donning a uniform and going off to war. So above the soda fountain a row of giant black and white photos of Glenn Miller's band marched along that wall.

A favor? What kind of favor? Betsy wondered.

"Good morning, Willie. What'll it be for you and your co-chair there?" The druggist smiled across the room at Betsy. "What are you two plotting to shake things up around here now?"

Betsy returned his smile. "We're open to suggestions," she said.

Willie came back carrying a tray of Coke glasses, straws, and long-handled spoons for extra stirring. Someone had put a quarter in the jukebox and Glenn Miller's band was playing *"A String of Pearls"* – good way to keep *their* conversation more private, Betsy thought.

"This is it in a nutshell, Betsy – before any of our friends come in and so you can get your groceries home."

She stirred the chocolate around in the Coke a few times, slowly, deliberately.

"I'm listening. . . ."

"Okay, look. I know you're not the only one wondering why Willie, the class clown, got himself into a serious project like this. I have my reasons. But I'm telling you and you alone. Mainly because you had the courage to do what I couldn't. Or chose not to. I mean, who'd bother to listen to what I'd say? And I could hardly believe you'd thought of it. And said it straight out and didn't let anyone talk you out of it. Do me the favor of keeping what I tell you between the two of us."

"Willie, you have my word." She looked him straight in the eyes.

"This is only your second year living in Plainsview, Betsy," Willie began, "and you might not know that I have two brothers older than me – Warren and Wally. Both gone away. Warren's in the Marines, serving on the Pacific Front."

Betsy drew in her breath. "No, I didn't know. How could I have missed seeing his name on the packages from home I take to the post office? Your family must be very worried."

He nodded, took a deep breath, and went on. "Wally – well, I don't know if you've heard about conscientious objectors, commonly referred to as COs..." he paused and looked at her.

The term "conscientious objector" was one she was scarcely aware of. And she'd never heard of anyone who actually had made that choice.

"Well, anyone who's a pacifist – like my brother Wally – they can land most anywhere from jail to serving without weapons overseas to the Civil Conservation Corps, the Forest Service, or to working in some hidden-away insane asylum. Wally's actually working in the Forest Service, but the U.S. soldier assigned to his unit is a real CO-hater and would rather be killing Nazis than supervising a bunch of cowards on some stupid forest improvement project. Draw your own conclusions about how he treats men he calls 'cowards.' If the men are marching through a town somewhere, they get spat on, kicked, called names."

Betsy had no idea such a thing was going on.

"As for my parents – they don't understand Wally's choice but they do stand by him. They believe Warren's doing the right thing.

But people here in Plainsview who know about Wally ignore what Warren's doing and – well, it's no surprise to find rotten eggs and tomatoes, cow manure, all sorts of trash all over our porch and windows and such. Always a hate note attached."

"Willie, I'm sorry. I didn't know...."

He waved her off. "I'm proud of both my brothers. When I was a little kid and some older boys started punching and kicking me, Warren showed up and took them to the principal. He wasn't much bigger than they were and he was only one and they were three, but they were scared of him. He did the same for Wally. And after Pearl Harbor what he wanted most was to fight for our country. Wally's brave in a different way. Whenever Wally caught bigger kids picking on me or calling me names, he stood between them and me and started asking them questions like what I did to make them want to hurt me. They'd stammer, look down at their feet and slouch off. When he saw a couple of kids fist-fighting in the alley, he did the same. And I couldn't figure out why they didn't turn around and bop him. When war was declared, he signed up as a CO. He believed someone had to stand up for resolving problems without tanks and bombs. Warren does it his way, Wally his – and each respects the other." He lifted his chin. "So, Betsy, you see it isn't just 'coloreds' or folks who don't 'talk American' here in town that get treated wrong. There's a list of wrongs to right – maybe nothing like a 'string of Pearls' but a string of prejudices, and I figure I'm going to work on one for starters, maybe by clowning around, maybe by standing behind you."

Betsy swallowed the lump in her throat. It was going to be hard not to tell Mom and Dad about this, to ask whether they knew about Willie's CO brother. But she'd given her word and she'd keep it.

At the prescription counter a couple of grownups picked up their packages and turned to leave. Jack Gordon came through the door with a bag of doughnuts from the bakery and walked up to the counter. "Your order, Pete," he said, handing him the bag. He called across to Willie and Betsy. "Gee, Betsy, you took a big chance leaving your bike out front... you sure Spud Sherman and his gang's got other things to do this morning?" He walked over and slid into the booth beside

Willie. "Got a big committee meeting going here, you two?"

Pete winked and said, "They've been in serious conversation there. Don't know what they'll be up to next, but I'm betting it's some project to better the community."

With Willie's story spinning inside her, Betsy set her glass aside, and stood to leave. "I'd better get these groceries home," she said.

Willie held her jacket for her, Jack grabbed her grocery bags. "These go in your bike basket, I take it?"

"They do, Jack, thanks." She turned to Willie. "And thanks, Willie. You're right. This committee does have more work to do."

And she had a lot of thoughts to process.

CHAPTER 17

Coming Home

Arms linked, Betsy and her friends blended with the crowd streaming into the high school gym. Superintendent Sievers and Principal Maxwell flanked the door, making sure no outsiders slipped in – only high school students and recent graduate service men and women home on leave – were allowed. Fred Hopper, too. Betsy was glad he was allowed even if he was out of school and not serving in the military. Fred's draft card could have read "A-1, serving on the home front." The jukebox was playing *"This is the Army, Mr. Jones,"* and a few kids were dancing, others standing around in small groups or finding a folding chair along the wall to sit on. Just inside the door the girls paused, stared at the dimly lit room – and beamed. Gone was the gym, the basketball floor shone smooth for dancing, crepe paper streamers in school colors cocooned the room in red and black, bright ceiling lights out of sight, a soft glow filtering the room, and strains of "I'll be seeing you. . . ." set the mood. On the wall above the refreshment table were framed photos of Plainsview grads in the service or working in war weapons plants with cut-out black letters spelling "Coming Home Soon." Em pointed out the photos of her brother, Ed, and sister, Midge.

Excitement charged the air – a major victory for the Warriors! What could make their homecoming game sweeter than beating the mighty Hawks? Just then Rosemary spotted Colleen, clinging to Blackie Hoffman's arm, acting like she owned him. He'd made the winning touchdown.

Fran gave a low-pitched wolf whistle. "She does look – well, like a beauty queen," Fran said, "I have to admit. That new pink angora sweater looks swell with her auburn hair. Too bad her personality doesn't match her looks."

"Gosh, kids – get a gander at the black patent high heels," Ruthie said. She couldn't help staring. "And I'll bet those stockings aren't nylon. They're sheer silk." No one had silk stockings any more, not the older girls or anybody's mothers. Not many even had nylons, newly invented on account of no more silk coming from the Far East. "Personally, though, I'll stick with bobby sox. Why fool with those irksome garter belts?"

"My aunt in Denver uses leg paint when she goes on a special date," Mary Beth said. "I've watched her do that a couple of times. The good thing is a straight line traced along the center of the back of each leg means you don't have to worry whether your seams are straight."

Betsy thought about her grandmothers having to settle for wearing cotton stockings during the war, Grandma Atwood's fastened to a corset, Grandma Blakesly's to a garter belt. No one went barelegged.

"Where do you suppose she got them – if they *are* silk?" Betsy wanted to know. Each of her grandmothers had a pair of silk hose wrapped in tissue paper in their cedar chests, the last before the war brought the silk shortage. Those came out only for a wedding or a funeral. Mom had one pair of nylons saved at the back of her dresser drawer to wear to church and for special occasions. She'd nearly cried when one of them snagged and got a small run, which she'd stopped with a dab of clear nail polish.

The girls looked at one another.

"Hmmm, well, either she persuaded her mother to wear a pair of hers that she was saving back or. . . ." Em left the sentence unfinished.

"Black market," Fran said it out loud. "I wouldn't put that past the Shermans."

"Oh, well, let's forget Colleen," Ruthie said. "We're here to dance. To celebrate our win and have fun!"

Em looked at Betsy. "My brother – Eddie – is home on leave, you know. He wants to meet you, Betsy."

Goosebumps prickled the skin of Betsy's arms. "Me? Why would he want to meet me?"

"For one thing I've told him what a swell kid you are," Em said, "and when I showed him the snapshot of us girls together, he pointed you out and said you were pretty cute."

Betsy felt her face flush and glanced away.

"Come on, Betsy," Fran said, "it's true you know. And you look really swell in that new jumper. I'm glad you broke down and sent off to *Calling All Girls* for it. And your long-sleeved white blouse makes you look at least sixteen."

Just then Chuck, soft-spoken in a firm way as always, tapped Rosemary on the shoulder. "May I have this dance?" he said, taking her by the hand, and called over his shoulder. "Great job on the decorations, girls!"

Fred Hopper limped over to Betsy. "Do you mind dancing with a guy whose draft card says he's 4-F on account of a bad leg? A slow number's coming up or I wouldn't have asked. Swing and jitterbug aren't in my repertoire."

"I'm not exactly Ginger Rogers myself, Fred." She smiled, remembering how Dad complained that kids today hadn't been taught ballroom dancing and didn't know the first thing about what real dancers do. Mom let him say his piece, then reminded him that their parents claimed that doing the Charleston in the '20s was corrupting young people, but they'd danced the Charleston all the same. Betsy relaxed, glad that Fred had asked before Jack, whose head loomed just beyond Fred.

And then everyone was dancing, lining up for punch at the refreshment table, laughing and talking in small groups that shifted and changed. With the lights low, it wasn't easy to tell but she and Fred counted three fellows in uniforms – two sailors and a soldier. Two others home on leave chose to dress in their "civies" – cord pants and V-neck wool sweaters.

Harry James' band was playing "It's been a long, long time...." and the dreamy notes put people in a sentimental mood. Teacher chaperones frowned at couples dancing too close – including Colleen and Blackie who were practically glued together, but Betsy could relax with Fred as her partner – he kept a distance between them and talked a bit.

"I guess about the only time we talk, Betsy, is when I'm painting names on the Honor Roll Board." He nodded toward the soldier. "It gives me a good feeling to see Dan Graves right here in the high school gym tonight, but the other part of me knows that he's home on leave because he'll be shipping out soon."

"We have to believe he'll be coming home again some day," Betsy said. "That's how I try to think about my cousin Johnny."

"Knowing he's missing has to be really tough for your family, all right. That word could mean so many things."

Just then a fellow in a sailor suit tapped Fred on the shoulder. "Introduce me to your dance partner, Fred," he said. "If I'm not mistaken, she's my sister Emily's friend."

Fred let go of Betsy's hand, turned. "You're right, Ed. Meet Betsy Blakesly, Betsy this is Emily's brother, Ed Mason."

Suddenly Betsy's pulse was racing – knew his eyes were taking her in. How old was he? Older than Em, younger than Midge but old enough to be drafted. She stole a glance at him in person – she'd seen Em's photo of him – the white of his sailor's suit set off a thick head of hair much darker than Em's light brown, dark eyes and eyebrows, square face, angular chin, taller than Fred but not as tall as Jack. What made her nervous was the way he was looking at her. No boy she knew had ever looked at her like that, she didn't know what it meant, but she couldn't meet that look.

And then they were dancing. Or rather he was, and she – feeling clumsier by the moment – was trying to follow.

"Hey, relax, Baby – relax and let me lead," he murmured in her ear.

They were in the middle of the floor, he'd steered her away from Fred and Jack wasn't in sight, either. He sure was a swell dancer, Betsy thought, knew how to thread smoothly through other couples – some of them girls dancing with girls and boys watching from the walls of the gym – so it surprised her when they bumped lightly against Colleen and Blackie. To Betsy it seemed a deliberate move. Both couples paused – Blackie and Ed apologizing, Colleen glaring, then pasting on a smile when she saw the sailor suit.

"Good to see you, Ed," Blackie said, and the fellows shook hands.

"Shipping out soon?"

Ed nodded. "One more week at home. Isn't your number coming up, too, Blackie?"

"Yeah. Maybe even before graduation. Can't wait to get in." He clasped Colleen's hand tighter. She nudged even closer.

"Great game tonight, buddy," Ed said, "and given the shape you're in, you're bound to sail through basic training."

Now the jukebox was playing *"Chattanooga Choo-Choo,"* couples who could jitterbugging, others stumbling over some version of it. Everyone celebrating the homecoming win. Betsy began to panic. Where was Em? Where were her friends? Where was Fred – and where was Jack when for once she really wanted him to show up?

"Let's get out of here, Betsy," Ed said, edging toward the door. "I need some fresh air."

"Leaving's not allowed." Betsy tried to loosen his hold on her hand without making a spectacle. "I mean, it's a school dance rule. Maybe it's okay for you since you're not a student and are home on leave and all... but if I leave, they won't let me back in."

"Oh relax, let yourself have some fun," Ed shoved into the corridor where all the coats were on hangers or thrown across tables. "What's breaking a stupid school rule gonna hurt? We can slip out and back in without anyone noticing."

He grabbed his pea jacket, picked up a girl's princess style coat with a soft brown fur collar. "This yours?"

She shook her head and pointed to her plain brown coat. Her heart raced. The two of them were alone in the hallway, and he was strong. If only the air raid siren would sound right now. Then the teachers would hustle them all to the basement, she'd find her friends and Eddie could grab one of the older and prettier girls. He'd forget about her.

Outside snow had begun to fall. Big flakes glittering under a glow of light from the school's outdoor lamppost – thick and wet, the sky reflecting back their whiteness. But Eddie was leading her around to the back of the building where it was darker and a few cars were parked, scarcely visible.

"Come on, Baby, let's get into my dad's car over here… we'll take a little spin around town. You know, like the song says, 'see all the familiar places.' It could be the last time I see them for who knows how long?" He opened the passenger door.

But she didn't get in. He leaned close, his breath on her face. He smelled of… after shave lotion? Hair oil? Something else? "I'm sorry, Ed, but I'm not allowed to get in the car with a fellow without my parents' approval," she said.

"Betsy, this is war time. I need to make every minute count. Come on, your dad's not going to find out." He was pressing against her now, gripping her elbow, forcing her.

"Please, no. I'm not the girl you want." Her voice came out strained, panicked.

She twisted away, but he pinned her arm behind her, holding tight.

Two figures emerged from the shadows. One of them grabbed and held Eddie, the other raised his fist and knocked the sailor out cold. Together the men shoved the unconscious figure into the back seat, opened the car window a little, and shut the door.

Turning, Betsy saw them full face. Caught her breath. They wore the blue denim P.O.W. outfits. What were they doing here? How had they gotten out of camp? She should run. They'd grab her next.

But the taller of the two took her gently by the elbow, touched his finger to his lips, began guiding her away, the other one looking up and down the street, peering into the snow. "Ve tak you home, Miss," he said. "Show vay, pliz."

She whispered. "But how – ? Why – ?" Strangely, she wasn't afraid of them. They weren't going to hurt her. Instead, she was afraid *for* them. Maybe they wanted to hide out in someone's basement, but what then? There was no place for them to go. And with the snow their footprints would give them away. What if they'd been missed back at camp? Were guards out searching?

The crunching of shoes on snow came from behind them, growing closer. And then Jack was there – he was fast on his feet – taking in the situation. He looked at the two men, they looked back at him. He looked at Betsy.

"What's happening here? I saw Ed Mason dancing with you, then edging you off the dance floor...so I went looking for you. I didn't want to butt in, but – well, I think he'd been drinking, Betsy, and I... well, I...."

The four of them kept walking, taking long strides, hugging the shadows, trying not to be seen or heard. "I don't know how they got here, Jack, but these fellows – well, they came to my rescue."

The second fellow explained, "Ve yust vanted to see vat the dance vas like. Vanted to...to...."

"I think I understand," Jack said. "I don't know how you managed to escape, but you're in bad trouble. You need to get back to the camp without anyone seeing you."

"No vorry," the first one said. "Ve have plan. Ve be okay. This girl need go home."

Jack said, "I'll get her there. You fellows have to hurry. Don't get caught!"

They looked at Jack, at Betsy, at each other, one said, "Okay, ve go."

Jack shook each of their hands. "My name's Jack. Thanks for rescuing my friend here – Betsy."

"I Helmut, this Gottfried. Ve thank you, too."

Betsy shook hands with each one, couldn't speak past the lump in her throat.

Their steps faded into the silence of snow, flakes shone like miniature stars in the corner streetlight outside the Blakeslys' house. Jack paused, looked down at Betsy, said, "We must speak of this to no one, agreed?"

She blinked tears from her eyes, managed to say, "Just between us. And, Jack. Thanks."

~

Even the hot water bottle Mom had tucked between the bed sheets couldn't stop her shivering, ease her to sleep. Soon after midnight, still tossing in a tangle of blankets, she heard Dad open the back porch door coming from his shift at the factory, the thump of his boots, and Mom going to the kitchen, making cocoa, Dad's voice gruff like it was when he got upset, Mom's voice rising. Betsy strained her ears and caught Dad's words – two P.O.W.s had been caught attempting to sneak into camp a couple of hours ago. A guard fired shots. The Dobermans tore into the escapees. Someone had spread the news at the factory: one prisoner dead, the second in the infirmary. No one knew yet how they'd gotten out or why.

"I'll check the furnace and the coal bin," Betsy heard Dad say. "Looks like we'll need heat in the morning with this snow coming down."

The last thing Betsy remembered hearing was the sound of Dad's work shoes on the basement stairs.

CHAPTER 18

When the Lights Go On Again

Mom's grocery list in her blue jeans pocket, Betsy pulled on the thick red sweater Grandma Adkins had knit and crossed Main Street. Already the Saturday morning sun was melting last night's snow, though heat when the furnace turned on at dawn had helped warm her body if not her spirits. If only sun could melt away the bad parts from the homecoming dance. Make it so it was all a bad dream. According to Dad, "Things always look better in the morning."

But not this morning. Oh, how she'd longed to bury her head in the warmth of her blanket, not put her bare feet on the cold floor and walk into the kitchen, fire answers to Cat's nosy questions, listen to Billie's million-times cheer for the team, invent an excuse for why she'd come home an hour and a half early. And bite her tongue not to let anything slip out about what happened with Ed and the war prisoners. Questions raged through her mind – was it Helmut or Gottfried who was dead? How bad were the other's injuries? She felt the need to put a name to each face. Then there was that disaster with Emily's brother, Ed. What could she possibly say when Em asked how she'd gotten along with Ed? And what *had* happened to Ed after Helmut and Gottfried stuffed him in the car? She hoped she'd never run into Emily's brother again. Ever. If she weren't such a nitwit... none of this would have happened and the German boy would still be alive. What else might Dad hear at the factory about the prisoners?

"Hi, Betsy!"

Betsy looked up. It was Joey Sullivan on the way to his shoeshine box at the barber's. "Hello there, Joey," she called back, telling herself that today was almost like all other Saturday mornings. Almost.

They waved to each other, and she noticed Fred Hopper setting up his ladder and pail of paint next to the Honor Roll board. He must have walked over from his job at the hardware store.

"I was hoping to claim another dance with you last night," he said when she got closer. "After all, we didn't ever finish that first one."

Betsy felt her face flush. "We'll make that up at the next school dance, Fred." She pointed at the board. He hadn't said anything about the prison camp escape. Maybe he hadn't heard the news yet. Or maybe he didn't want to scare her. She sure didn't want to talk about the dance, though, and changed the subject. "More names to add?"

"More almost every day," he answered and named three new draftees... the last was supposed to graduate in May. Would Blackie be next? Betsy wondered.

"I've got errands to do for my mom, Fred," she said. "Be careful on that ladder."

"Hey, Mr. Perfect Balance, that's me," he said and waved her off.

She paused at the door to the post office and took three deep breaths. What kind of talk was going on there?

"Mornin', Betsy." Mr. Mason glanced up from sorting the mail. She called good morning back, relieved that he hadn't tried to make conversation about homecoming. She stayed close to the wall leading to the rows of postal boxes.

"Served 'em right," Mr. Slipher was saying to the huddle of men standing near the *"Uncle Sam Wants You!"* poster. "Oughta line 'em all up in front of a firing squad."

Mr. Sherman pounded a fist in the palm of his other hand. "Save the country a lot of money – and clean our house of Krauts at the same time."

"Not to mention making us all safer. Specially the women folks," growled Hank Schiff, who must have come to town with his wife for Saturday shopping.

"All two thousand, going on three?" Pete Taylor questioned, moving toward his post office box. "What makes you think killing off the prisoners is going to solve the world's problems?" He didn't wait for an answer.

"Just what we need," Mr. Van Brandt said under his breath. "Another lecture from our resident professor of war."

Betsy hurried past the men, hoping they wouldn't notice her.

But Mr. Slipher looked right at her. "So, girlie," he called, "what do you say about those Nazis sneaking out of the camp last night?"

Betsy looked at him a moment. "My name is Betsy, Mr. Slipher, as you may remember from our talk a few weeks ago about designating non-white customers to balcony seats at the movies." *(To herself she noted – rusty seats with a poor view but full price tickets.)*

He guffawed. "People should know their places and stay there." He looked around for approval from the other three, who halfway nodded but shifted their feet and didn't look at Betsy.

"So you pointed out to me. Without any discussion. As for what I think about the prisoners' escape, I don't know enough about it to form an opinion." She turned and headed for their mailbox, twirled the knob with the lock code, and pulled out a handful of letters – one a V-mail – the latest *Saturday Evening Post*, then emptied Helen Martin's box of its contents. She couldn't get out of here fast enough.

At the Mercantile Mary Beth was just leaving with a bag of groceries. "Betsy! What happened to you last night? When it was time to go, no one knew where you were. It was like the snow had swallowed you up."

Betsy stammered. "Sorry, Mary Beth. I should have let one of you know. I. . . ."

"Ah-ha! Did Em's brother sweep you off somewhere? We didn't see him anywhere, either."

Her stomach was churning. "Oh, no, nothing like that. I just – well, I felt like, well, you know, it's that time of the month, and. . . ."

Mary Beth's tone softened, "Gee, Betsy, what a time for that to happen. I'm sorry you missed most of the dance, and you in your new jumper, too." Her brow furrowed. "You feeling okay today?"

They looked around, moved to a quieter place near the door. There was a lot of animated chatter going on among the shoppers. They wouldn't be paying attention to a couple of whispering teenagers.

Betsy shrugged. "Not exactly 'swell,' but an aspirin helps. "

"Well, it's a relief to know you got home without those prisoners grabbing you or something else awful. You have heard what happened, haven't you?"

"I heard that some prisoners somehow got out of the camp and then got caught trying to get back inside. And...."

"Two prisoners, it seems. The guards killed one and wounded the other." Mary Beth hugged herself, grocery bag and all, and shivered.

"What does it all mean?" Betsy wondered.

"Guess we'll learn more. But I've got to get these groceries home and I know you need to get your chores done, too. See you tomorrow in your choir robe?"

"Sure. Maybe we'll know more then. But you have to wonder how much of what people say is real and how much is just gossip."

Mary Beth rolled her eyes. "The kind of thing Mrs. Slipher's famous for. Best to wait till the Denver newspapers or the radio broadcasts do their investigating."

"And the *Sun* doesn't come out till Thursday. Mr. Ray's sure to tell more of the story than the *Post* or the *News*, but it's hard not knowing any details." Betsy wanted to know now, but even then she knew the prisoners' names wouldn't be printed. She might never know whether it was Helmut or Gottfried who wouldn't be shipped home after the war. She felt sick all over.

"So, Betsy, how did you happen to snag Em's brother for a dance last night?"

Startled, Betsy had narrowly missed bumping into Colleen.

She shrugged. "Luck, maybe. Can't stop to talk. I'm on my way to the cash register."

"Luck? Maybe. But I'd bet Emily put him up to that. He's kinda cute, isn't he, in that sailor suit and all?"

"I noticed he gave *you* a long look." Betsy steered the subject to Colleen *(naturally, Colleen's mind was on the dance, not the prison shooting talk going on everywhere else in the store).* "And why wouldn't he?" Betsy called over her shoulder, "You looked like a pinup girl in that new dress."

It was a relief to talk to Mr. George at the cash register. He glanced around, reached under the counter, slipped bananas into her sack. No other customers were likely to hear. "Saved these back for your mother, Betsy. I've added them to the Blakesly charge account."

"Gee, thanks, Mr. George." She kept her voice low. "It's sure been a long time since we tasted bananas."

"Just between the two of us – sure too bad about those boys out at the camp," he said, "I can't think they meant any harm, but it's sure put the town in a frenzy."

"What must being locked inside that camp all the time feel like? It's hard to know what not to fear any more."

Mr. George nodded. "Like our President said, 'We have nothing to fear but fear itself.' But we fear everything anyway. And this war seems like it's never going to end."

He clipped out the correct food rationing stamps, gave her the copy of the amount he'd charged to Dad's account. When she was younger, Betsy liked walking with Mom (in her best housedress) up and down Main Street the first day of each month to pay their bills. Now it was Billie who got to do that.

He turned when Mrs. Newsom approached, ready for him to ring up her bill and bag her groceries.

"Good Morning, Betsy," Mrs. Newsom said. "My, wasn't that a fine game last night?"

Always glad to see Mrs. Newsom, Betsy was happier still to talk about the game instead of the prisoners. At the same time, though, she wondered whether the care package ladies would be baking cinnamon rolls at Doc Wendling's request. If they did and their friend Bill was the soldier on guard when she and Jack got there, maybe he'd tell them the name of the prisoner being treated. She just had to know. To say his name in her prayers. She wondered if the lights would ever come on again all over the world like the song said.

At the bakery, her last stop, Jack took her order, then lowered his voice. "You okay this morning, Betsy?"

She nodded, forced a smile. "I'm okay. I just wish – it hadn't happened."

"Anything else?" Jack asked loudly enough for his boss to hear and rang up the sales.

Betsy handed him the correct change. "Thanks, and come back soon." He lowered his voice again. "We did what we could, you know, but...." and his voice choked a little, too. On her way out Betsy realized this was the first time ever that he hadn't teased her about her order. Or anything else.

CHAPTER 19

The Chattanooga Choo-Choo?

S he didn't want to go to school, didn't want not to go to school. The weekend hadn't helped calm the churning inside her, hadn't slowed that freight train of homecoming dance nightmares chasing beneath the details of two "normal" day by day routines. If only this train's destination were the same as that of the *"Chattanooga Choo-Choo,"* she thought, a train that would "carry *her* home," locking every last scrap of bad news in the baggage car. If only.

There was nothing for it but to go on as if nothing had happened, to just get through the day. Being on duty at the savings stamps sales booth with Rosemary helped. She could rely on Rosemary to be a calm, steady presence.

They arrived early and got the booth set up. "Well, kid," Rosemary said, handing Betsy sheets of stamps – mostly the 10 and 25 cent kind (half dollar, dollar, and five dollar ones were beyond the pocketbooks of teenagers) along with stamp books that could be traded for an E-bond when filled. She began organizing the moneybox and record book, "I don't see how the teachers can expect us to focus on school work after all that happened Friday night."

Betsy shook her head. "Nothing feels anywhere near 'normal' to me. Maybe Mr. Maxwell will say something about it before first period starts."

"I hope he does," Rosemary said, then leaned closer as kids began streaming through the school door. "And, Betsy, I think we should have at least three people on the school paper staff write opinion articles – maybe one person from each class, a sophomore, junior, and senior."

"Definitely," Betsy agreed. "I'm sure the staff will come up with the right people – and we can count on Miss Price for good advice." She told herself to match Rosemary's sense of calm, to set her worries aside.

Looking up, she saw Emily walk through the door, head for the stamp booth. The pit of Betsy's stomach turned stone cold. She busied her hands straightening the stack of stamp books.

"Eddie thinks you're a swell kid, Betsy. A nice girl, kind of shy." She put down five dimes, Betsy counted out five savings stamps.

"He sure is a good dancer," Betsy said. "Your family must be worried about having him ship out." *What would it be like down deep in the ocean, likely the Pacific, shut up inside a submarine? She hadn't been very nice to him, and now....*

"Sure are," Em nodded without looking up, slipped the stamps inside her book. Lowering her voice she said, "He's in the doghouse with the folks, though. Thinks he has to 'live it up' his last few days home." Moving away for the next person in line, she called, "Talk to you later."

What did Em mean by "talk"? Betsy wanted in the worst way to know in what shape Eddie was when he got home Friday night, what he'd made of finding himself passed out and alone in the car, not remembering who'd knocked him out and why. Was his jaw swollen? Bruised? Maybe even bandaged for a split chin or something? She hadn't seen him around town or at church – and was relieved about that, but still she hoped he was okay and wanted to know for sure he hadn't seen who hit him. It was awfully dark, but still – Guilt, sadness, regret washed through her all over again. But that was something else she must keep to herself. She hated "secrets." And these were the darkest she'd ever known. Honesty was a rule at the Blakesly home. She wasn't telling any lies, but somehow not telling the whole truth felt the same as a lie. Was it? Or was the "right" thing not all that clear sometimes?

Rosemary nudged her. "Your mind's drifting."

Betsy willed herself to focus on selling stamps, glanced at the clock – two minutes till the first bell and Rosemary was putting the money in the safe deposit bag for Mrs. Greene to lock in the safe.

The girls closed the booth and joined the crowd streaming into the auditorium. Plainsview High's auditorium served multiple purposes – homeroom to all three grades, study hall, assembly, and concerts and plays. Instead of theatre seats, rows of desks stretched to the back of the room from below the wide, curtained stage. Sophomores and juniors sat in assigned desks flanking the seniors in the center – each student stored their books in the wide lift up desktop and reported there first thing every morning. For special evening concerts and plays grownups and kids alike squeezed by twos or more into each desk.

On this Monday morning everyone sat in place, eyes focused as usual on Mr. Maxwell who led students and faculty in the pledge to the flag, then read out the schedule for the day. In an attempt to keep her hands from trembling, Betsy folded them across the books she'd pulled out for her first two classes, biology and geometry. Two of her hardest subjects, guaranteed to make her concentrate on studies, not "extra curricular" topics. Or so she hoped.

The bell rang for first period classes. But Mr. Maxwell held up his hand before anyone had a chance to move. "Classes will start a few minutes late this morning," he said and waited for silence. A sense of expectation rippled through the auditorium.

"I'm certain you've all heard about the incident involving two war prisoners Friday night. Some of what you've heard is probably factual, some should be labeled 'rumors,' and others 'invented' to make a good story."

The room was so silent that if someone were to drop a handkerchief, it would sound louder than a bass drum.

"The undercurrent beneath all this talk is – Fear," Mr. Maxwell went on. "People are wondering things like – Are we safe? What happens if more prisoners escape camp? Should we stay home and lock all the doors and windows?"

He paused, knew he had everyone's full attention. His was a deep voice, not as deep as Dad's, Betsy thought, or as growly the way Dad's got when he was angry or worried – rather, it was deep in a commanding sort of way just bordering the edges of threatening.

"Now. First I want you to know that no one at school or all of Plainsview is in danger. So don't waste time or energy on fear. Instead, re-double the energy you put into mastering your school-work and on your war effort projects. That's what counts in getting this war won sooner. That's when the prisoners will be shipped back to their own countries, the camp itself dismantled, and the land farmed again."

Easy for him to say, Betsy thought, but that sure didn't answer the questions she wanted answers to.

"The officials at the camp aren't allowed to make much information public, but what I can tell you is that the two young men shot trying to get back inside the gates had probably slipped off the truck that was driving the group of prisoners back after the homecoming game. The soldiers on guard didn't miss them till they got back to camp and took roll call. When the beacon lights shone on the men scrambling to climb over the fence, the guards in the watchtowers did what they'd been trained to do and fired their guns. Of course the watchdogs, too, obeyed their training and went on attack. That's how the tragedy occurred. Neither prisoner was considered dangerous or he would not have been allowed to go to the game. Every prisoner in the camp who's considered dangerous will never step outside the gates of the high fence to work in the fields or at the sugar factory. And every guard at the camp is exercising tight security."

He paused, then asked, "Are there any questions?"

A hand from the section for juniors shot up.

Mr. Maxwell nodded. "Yes, Leonard."

Leonard stood, cleared his throat. "There's some talk around town that we're being too soft on the prisoners, Mr. Maxwell," he said.

"Yes, I've heard that too, Leonard. We're all quick to judge when we think things aren't fair. But the Army makes the rules. They have the big picture, ours is no bigger than a snapshot."

Leonard pressed on. "But if we are being soft here and that puts us in danger, shouldn't they get more strict?"

Betsy had to admire Leonard for persisting even if she didn't know what to think about how the prisoners should be treated. She'd never have the nerve to speak up to Mr. Maxwell.

"I'm sure that issue's been brought up to the camp officials, Leonard, and no doubt now will be again. But, as I said, we don't know the whole picture. They do. They're doing what they believe is in everyone's best interests."

Leonard sat down. No one else's hand went up.

"You're dismissed for class, but if anyone wants to talk further with me, you're welcome to come to the office during your free time."

Chuck caught up with Betsy in the corridor. "The committee needs to meet again. Today if possible, tomorrow noon at the latest. We have to find a way to ward off some of the hate talk going on."

Betsy nodded. "We sure do."

Chuck touched her shoulder. "I'll get a time from Mrs. Frei, then we can tell the others. I'll split the list with you and Willie."

"Thanks, Chuck." Betsy smiled and strode toward Room 204. It was the first real smile she'd smiled for three days, she realized, and felt some of the weight of that heavy freight train lighten ever so little. Something like the lines from the song, "coming in on a wing and a prayer."

CHAPTER 20

And Bless Thy Good with Brotherhood

"Willie will explain why we're having this meeting," Betsy said. "We don't have much time, so we'll get right down to it."

They'd made a half circle of the armchair desks at the front of Mrs. Frei's room and closed the door to shut out the lunch hour noise in the hall.

Shifting his weight from foot to foot, Willie cleared his throat, stared at the floor, then squared his shoulders and looked into five faces, each one curious and eager. Betsy held her breath, hoping the infamous class clown wouldn't fall back into one of his annoying tricks like cracking his knuckles or wiggling his oversized ears.

"The reason we're meeting," he stammered, "is – well, it's on account of... on account of the bad talk around town. About the prison escape."

Betsy relaxed, astonished at how being on this committee had somehow brought out a side of Willie she'd never have guessed.

Glenn's hand shot up. "But weren't we just going to...."

Rosemary interrupted, something she didn't often do. Her voice quiet as always, yet firm. "Something tells me that the initial purpose of our committee was only a beginning. We may have unlocked some sort of Pandora's box."

"Maybe so. But looking at where all this could lead is one thing," Leland cautioned. "Actually getting anything done about it is another. I mean, we didn't even manage to talk every business owner into taking down their 'whites only' signs." He paused, then went on. "Exhibit A: Mr. Harvey P. Sly-pher at the movie theatre."

Leland made it sound like he'd changed the "i" in Slipher to a "y" – like all the kids did, silently if not out loud. Behind his back, of course.

Chuck ignored the slur. "That's true," he acknowledged. "But that doesn't mean we failed. The committee – and our class – did meet the goal. After all, we brought the issue of injustice out of hiding. Got people talking. And thinking." He looked around, saw the nods of agreement, motioned toward Willie. "So, Willie, tell us."

"Sure, we started out with one goal – getting those signs down," Willie said, confidence growing in his manner and his voice. "But how could we have guessed then what happened Friday night with the escaped prisoners disaster and all the ruckus it's stirred up? Like talk at the post office – 'Line 'em all up in front of a firing squad' – 'Ship all them Krauts out' – So first we need to decide whether addressing the issue is something our committee should take on. And if it is, what are some ways we could try to make it work?"

"Maybe it'll just die out on its own," Glenn suggested. "You know how people drop one piece of gossip when something else pops up to talk about. If we butt in, that could just make the hate talk get worse and last longer."

Betsy could hardly sit still. "But if we don't try to cool things down, if we don't try to get them to listen to reason, there could be a group that would decide to make things even worse for the prisoners than cutting back their rations and the small privileges they get like what happened during harvest."

"Which, after all," Chuck pointed out, "follow the rules of war for how countries treat prisoners of war. Some people need to study the rules. Or at least read them."

"And who makes sure that Germany, Italy, and Japan follow the rules?" Glenn pointed out.

"Look," Rosemary said, "let's keep the problem right here for now. We can bring those other things up later."

Yes, Betsy silently agreed, wanting to get on with it. She couldn't erase the newsreel running through her mind: images of the fellows in their blue denim prison outfits emerging from the night shadows and risking their own safety to help her when she didn't know how to help herself, walking her home in the snow, then Jack coming along and the four of them exchanging names before Jack urged the runaways back to the camp... and then... and then the news they'd been shot trying to climb over the high barbed wire fence. It was all her fault. She'd never, ever get over it! And now she had to do something – anything – to try to make it up to them.

Willie was talking again. "And we already know how angry some people are about how much better the prisoners have it than we do," he said. His freckles seemed to turn a darker shade.

Leland frowned. "We could be getting ourselves into something we shouldn't." He shook his head and ran the palms of his hands across the top of his thick brown crew cut.

"But if we don't," Rosemary said, biting her lower lip, "what will we think of ourselves? That we've got high ideas about erasing injustice – but we're too cowardly to actually do anything about it?"

"Looks like I'm not going to win any awards for bravery in the line of duty, Rosie," Leland conceded. "So. You win. But what can we do to really make a difference here?"

Chuck, leaning against the teacher's desk, smacked a fist on his palm. "That's exactly the question, Leland." He glanced at the clock on the wall. "Okay then, let's throw some ideas out on the table. Whatever comes to mind. Nothing's stupid or dumb. The point is to generate a list, look at it, and see what kind of plan we can come up with."

Rosemary poised her sharpened pencil over a sheet of blank notebook paper. "Make posters with some short, catchy mottos – like the war posters," she said, writing that down in her perfect penmanship.

"Put them in store windows, the Carnegie library and school libraries." That from Glenn, the incurable bookworm.

"Articles in the school paper?" Betsy ventured.

"Talks to clubs." Leland looked at Chuck. "Chuck should be the one for that."

"Bring it up wherever we go," Chuck said. "Turn gossip upside down."

"Get churches on our side," Rosemary chimed in.

"Student Council." Glenn's forehead furrowed.

"Kites and balloons could get their attention. Have fun with it." Willie should know, Betsy thought, smiling approval.

Ideas bounced off the walls, Rosemary resorted to practicing her lessons in shorthand, Chuck nodded his head and smiled, Mrs. Frei beamed. The bell was about to ring and people gathered their books.

Betsy announced they'd meet again right after school to come up with a plan of action – everyone but Leland, who had to catch the school bus. Willie volunteered to catch Leland between classes to get his ideas. Betsy hurried into the hall, her mind swirling like a cement mixer – running over what had been said at the meeting, heavy with guilt about Helmut and Gottfried whose faces were so young and – well, like any American boys – and daring to hope Mrs. Newsom would be baking rolls for the patients at the camp hospital, embarrassment about her stupid behavior with Em's brother, Eddie, and more immediately, mentally reviewing the Latin assignment. . . .

Then Jack tapped her on the shoulder, startling her back from that turmoil of worries. "Betsy," he said, "I know you don't want to be late to class, but some girl's crying in the rest room. Maybe you should take a look."

"Oh, Jack. . . ," Betsy protested. He was going to make her tardy to class and besides that – golly, what else could go wrong and what in the world could she do about it?

Jack nudged her. "I'll stop by your class and explain that you've been delayed. I've got study hall myself, so I won't be missing anything."

Against her will, Betsy pushed open the door to the girls' room and stepped inside. There stood Colleen Sherman leaning over one of the sinks, sloshing water over her face with water. And sobbing as if her heart would break.

CHAPTER 21

Loose Lips Sink Ships

Instinctively, Betsy rushed to Colleen's side, reached a hesitant hand toward the heaving shoulder.

"Gee, kid, what's wrong? Can I help?" She took a step back, thinking she was probably the last person on earth Colleen wanted to see, let alone touch. Especially now when the school's queen of beauty sure wasn't looking her shining best.

Betsy pulled out her handkerchief and handed it to Colleen. "Use it," she said. "It's clean."

Colleen dabbed at her swollen eyes, her puffy cheeks, choked down a few sobs. "Don't mind me," she muttered, trying to take control of herself. "I'll be okay in a few minutes."

"But something's making you cry. Are you sick? Do you want me to walk with you to the nurse's room? Have the office call your mother?" Betsy was at a total loss. Besides, she was going to be really late for Latin II class.

Colleen shook her head with an emphatic "No," and at the mention of the word "mother," a fresh flood of tears erupted. "S-s-sorry... I c-can't t-talk...."

Betsy put her hand on Colleen's shoulder again. Gently. "That's okay, kid. Nobody can talk and cry at the same time. Anyway, you don't have to talk at all. Go ahead and cry. I'll leave you alone if you want."

"S-s-stay. Please stay," Colleen said, blowing her nose and gulping for air. "Just for a bit." And she did seem to calm down ever so little.

And then – sometimes in bits and pieces, other times pouring out in a rush of words – Betsy patched the story together. Or at least a part of the story. What it came down to was that somehow the Shermans had found out that Colleen had disobeyed their orders never to associate with any boy from Mill Town, that she'd been seen holding hands with Blackie Hoffman. Naturally, Colleen thought she'd kept it a secret from her parents – kids at Plainsview High did things like going to the movies and ball games and dances in groups, not pairing off like going on a real date or something. But of course Colleen and Blackie always managed to sit next to each other at the movies, dance every dance with each other. It was plain to see they had a crush on each other. But as anyone in Plainsview knows, nobody can keep a secret here. And when the Shermans confronted Colleen, she didn't deny it. Instead she refused to stop seeing him.

"They don't even try to listen to reason." Colleen cast a pleading look at Betsy. "Blackie's not like the other folks in Mill Town. If my parents paid attention to anything but their own precious 'reputation,' they'd know that Blackie has the highest grade average in the senior class, that he's senior class president, captain of the football team, voted Homecoming King. And they couldn't be bothered to know things like giving every penny he earns to his father, same as his brother and sisters do. And since my parents are so persnickety about manners – Blackie's got the best manners of anyone I know. And considerate? How many kids are as good to their younger brother as he is? What does it matter where his parents came from or where they live now?"

Betsy wanted to say that Blackie wasn't the only one in Mill Town who was as good or better than people on this side of Mill Town. And that not everyone on this side of town was top notch, either. But she kept quiet. Colleen, for the first time Betsy since had known her, had let her guard down – and didn't have her nose in the air like usual.

"Please don't tell anyone, kid," Colleen pleaded. "It's none of their business – *(her nose went up in the air again like her old self)* "and I sure don't want anyone's pity."

Betsy gave her word. Oh, fiddlesticks! Another secret to keep, but Plainsview gossip line or not, Betsy vowed to keep hers from getting out. Now here she was with a new secret. One that left her feeling confused, filled her with mixed emotions somewhere between wanting to gloat – like *"Ha! So much for Colleen's high and mighty self!"* – at one end of the pole and on the other trying to imagine herself in Colleen's situation.

"When I stood up to them," Colleen went on, "they – they...." Here came a new burst of tears. She swallowed them back. Her voice lowered. "They told me I wasn't their daughter any more and to leave the house and never come back."

Betsy stood paralyzed. How could Colleen's parents – anybody's parents – say such a thing? What could she do? Where could she go? After all, she wasn't even sixteen yet.

"And that bratty little brother of mine." Colleen's face flushed with anger. "Do you think he'd stand up for me? No. He just stood there with a smirk on his fat freckled face and made that childish 'shame on you' sign."

That didn't surprise Betsy. To her it seemed Spud was born mean. Still, it made her sad. Shouldn't siblings stick up for each other?

"I'm so sorry," Betsy said, trying to hold her own feelings back. "What are you going to do? Does Blackie know yet?"

Colleen shook her head No, then lifted her chin. "I wanted to get myself under control first. But I have no idea where to go." She seemed to get a grip on herself, pulled out her comb and lipstick, and faced the mirror. "But I can't just stand here being a bawl baby, so I guess...."

Betsy couldn't leave her like this. She needed to do something. "I think the best thing to do now is get you to the nurse's room where you can be alone." She took Colleen gently by the elbow. "Miss Grant will let you lie down and rest. I promise you can trust her. Maybe she'll help you sort things out."

All at once Colleen's shoulders sagged. "Maybe you're right, Betsy. I just can't think straight right now."

The hall seemed strangely quiet with everyone in class. Betsy paused at the secretary's desk. Mrs. Greene's eyebrows lifted in a question, Betsy told her where they were going.

Climbing the stairs to the second floor, Betsy paused before they went in, turned to Colleen, blurted, "Look, kid. I'll come get you after school. Don't leave, okay? I'll be late on account of a committee meeting. But if you need a place to go tonight, you can come home with me."

CHAPTER 22

Let a Smile Be Your Umbrella

O n her way back to class, Betsy stopped at the office, reported that Colleen was with Miss Grant, and asked to use the phone to call her mother. "No, Mom, nothing's wrong with me... I can't explain just now, but – well, would it be okay if I bring Colleen Sherman home? She needs a place to spend the night – and, well, it's private – I know it's a school night, but – ? Thanks, Mom."

She didn't dare say more than that right here in the school office. But what was Mom to think? After all, Betsy and Colleen weren't exactly friends, especially not the kind of friend she'd ask to stay overnight. And never on a school night. How had she gotten herself into another stupid mess?

Betsy's stomach had been tied in knots all afternoon. Now she hurried into Mrs. Frei's room, put her books on a desk top and sat down, relieved that Willie would lead the meeting again and that Chuck was there, too. He and Mrs. Frei had gotten Mr. Maxwell's okay to take this project on.

"I caught up with Leland between classes," Willie began, skipping the formalities and picking up where they'd left off this noon. "He volunteered to be chief poster-maker. He'll get a couple of kids from his art class to help. But we need ideas for posters."

Rosemary's hand went up. "How about something like *'Kill Hate with Kindness'*? Or maybe *'Kindness Kills Hate'*? Could Leland create a simple poster from something like that?"

"Leland's got a real flair for art," Glenn said. "I'm betting he could. And maybe something that goes like *'Words As Weapons – War or Peace'*? And then there's our President's maxim – *'We have nothing to fear but fear itself.'*"

Betsy had her mind fully on the meeting now and offered another idea. "What about *'Faces of Peace'* as the opposite of the *'Faces of War'* poster? But I sure couldn't design a poster that captures those slogans." In her own mind, though, her cousin Johnny's face was the one she saw – knowing how she wanted him treated if he were in some German prisoner-of-war camp.

"That's Leland's job. He'll come up with something really swell," Willie said. "Now – about getting some articles in the school paper, a good place to start might be with some testimonials. Just a few sentences. Like from Doc Wendling and Mr. Maxwell and maybe one of the farmers. You know, grownups who've had some face-to-face contact with prisoners." He looked at Betsy. "Your dad, too, at the sugar factory."

Mrs. Frei stepped away from the windows where she'd been standing and cautioned, "Remember, though, that in an article you need to show all sides of an issue. Do your research thoroughly and let the readers make up their own minds."

"Gosh, I hadn't thought about that," Willie said, wrinkling his nose. "I guess you're right, but – well, our purpose is to change the attitude of certain people."

Glenn laid his pencil on his desk, seemed to be turning thoughts over in his head. "Maybe telling all sides can strengthen our argument, not kill it."

"It's what we've been preaching, after all," Rosemary pointed out. "About ignorance – lack of knowledge – causing fear and hate and name-calling. So we need to let the full story speak for itself."

Chuck glanced at the clock. "Good work, everyone," he said. "But it's time to go – football practice, after-school jobs, get going on your committee assignments. So, Rosemary, please write down who's going to interview which people and we'll go from there."

~

Cat stared bug-eyed when she spotted Colleen walking up the sidewalk with Betsy. Betsy shot Cat a warning frown and shook her head. Could Cat for once keep her big mouth shut?

Mom met them at the back door with a smile, welcomed Colleen, exchanged looks with Betsy, motioned them into the kitchen where a plate of apple slices and graham crackers spread with peanut butter waited on the table. Billie was on the floor, putting away his toy airplanes and tanks.

Betsy took Colleen's fur-trimmed white wool coat and hung it on a back porch hanger, then hung her own navy blue pea jacket beside it and joined Mom and Colleen in the kitchen.

"Sit down, girls," Mom said, ladling cocoa into cups and adding a fat marshmallow to each. "I'm sure I hear those after-school tummies growling."

Cat barged in, slamming the porch door behind her, caught Mom's frown and went back to close the door *qui-et-ly*. "Wait for me," she said, taking the chair across the table from Colleen. Betsy knew Cat was squirming to know what was going on. But she'd been taught her manners and up to now was remembering to use them.

Betsy helped Billie onto his stool. Mom sat in her usual place at the end of the table near the stove. Cat passed the plate of graham crackers and apple slices to Colleen.

When everyone had helped them selves, Mom looked at Cat and then Billie. "Children, Betsy's classmate, Colleen, will be our guest tonight. She's a guest, but it's a school night – not a party, so we'll keep on with our family routine."

She took a sip from her teacup, looked at Colleen. "Colleen, we're glad to welcome you. And here's how we'll work this out. Betsy's room is small – barely room for twin beds and a small chest of drawers – but that's where you'll be staying."

Betsy's heart sank. Share the only private space she had with – Colleen Sherman, of all people – this was going to be a horrible night. How was she supposed to act? Would she have to let Colleen wear her only other pair of pajamas? What about underwear? They weren't even close to the same size. Thank goodness she didn't wear lipstick or she'd have to share that, too. Except lipstick was one thing Colleen did have with her. As for one more person wanting to use the bathroom – holy cow! And what about her bedtime ritual of writing in her diary? She wasn't about to do that with Colleen in the same room.

Right now she thought she'd burst if she didn't write out her nightmares about Helmut and Gottfried. Which reminded her – she was supposed to interview Dad about his personal experiences with the prisoners assigned to the factory. How could she do that with Colleen in the house? Colleen was the type to think all the prisoners should face the firing squad. It was like a black cloud was hanging over her head.

"Each of you needs practice time before supper," Mom went on reciting her litany. Turning to Colleen, she said, "You can practice your saxophone in Betsy's room for half an hour, then come to the kitchen and help Cat set the supper table."

"*Mom-mie!*" Billie shrilled, climbing down from his stool. "That's my job. I know where everything's supposed to go." He stared straight at Mom.

"Okay, Billie, you're right," Mom said with a sigh. "So now I'm going to give you a more important job. You teach Colleen how we set the table at our house."

Billie puffed up with importance, his pout turning to a smile.

Tying on a fresh apron, Mom continued, "Betsy, you peel potatoes and carrots while Colleen practices, then it's your turn to practice." She looked at all of them then. But what she said was mostly for Colleen's instruction. "Dad will get home around 5:30, supper's at six – and also Edward R. Murrow's radio broadcast so we can hear the latest war news. Everyone helps clean up the kitchen after supper, then it's homework time. Bed time for Cat and Billie is 8 o'clock and for you girls it's lights out at 9."

House rules. My mom the organizer, Betsy realized, smiling to herself. She stole a glance at Colleen. Her face was blank, devoid of any emotion or thought. Or maybe, like Betsy herself, all Colleen could do was wonder what she'd gotten herself into. Still, Betsy thought Colleen's mind was made up and she wouldn't back down from what she'd told her parents. She was used to having her own way.

Dishes washed, wiped, and put away, kitchen floor swept, Cat and Billie trotted off to brush their teeth and wash their faces, pull on their pajamas, and join the rest of the family. Dad, in his favorite chair, was reading the evening paper, Billie curled up beside Mom for his story time. Cat had some homework to do, too, and joined the older girls at the table. By then Colleen and Betsy had finished translating the assigned Latin passages, filling out their English grammar worksheets, and now were outlining the next chapter in their history book – so boring! When they opened their geometry books, Dad put down the newspaper and walked over – on call for help. He seemed to have been born with numbers in his head and seemed to think Betsy was, too. He couldn't understand why those geometry terms and figures you made with tools like compasses and triangles and rulers, trying to measure distances like the diameter of a given circle were like a foreign language to her. The biggest mystery of all in Betsy's mind – those story problems. Last year she hadn't needed help with algebra. Miss Bruner explained everything so clearly and made sure each person in the class mastered one step before moving to the next. But geometry – she needed Dad to explain the lesson again at night. His patience was on the thin side, too – he kept repeating things like, "Use your head. It's just common sense." And then he'd go over whatever theorem or hypothesis or problem it was again. Betsy always ended up trying to hold back the tears and feeling really, really stupid. But still – if it weren't for Dad's help, she'd flunk the class.

And now tonight in front of Colleen, who perked up at Dad's pointers and right away figured out the solutions while Betsy sat there chewing on her pencil like a dummy, she resented Colleen even more. It wasn't fair.

Betsy managed to interview Dad while Colleen was in the bath-room. Promptly at nine o'clock, Betsy and Colleen were tucked into their beds when Mom slipped into the room to say Good Night and shut off the light.

Now that her homework was done – and she'd gotten Dad's views on the German prisoners *("anecdotes tell the story," she'd learned in journalism class)* – Betsy calmed down a bit. She turned toward the bed next to hers. "Feeling any better?" she whispered.

"I do feel better." Colleen swallowed hard, dodged the issue of her parents. "Gee, your dad's a whiz at math. Wish he were our teacher instead of that numbskull we've got." The room's silence deepened,

Colleen's tone changed and she said, "I'll never stop seeing Blackie. No matter what." She rolled on her side, away from Betsy.

After breakfast the next morning, Mom took the girls aside. "Colleen, Miss Grant phoned and wants you to report to her office first thing."

Wearing his cream-colored cords and long-sleeved blue work shirt, Dad whistled his way through the kitchen, and slipping on his jacket and cap, took the lunch Mom had packed for him. "Good work on those geometry problems, girls. Show those fellows in the class you're every bit as good at numbers and figures as they are." He shut the back porch door behind him. *Quietly.*

Mom walked the girls to the door, put her hand on Colleen's shoulder. "You're welcome to stay here till something can be worked out, dear."

Colleen looked away, then pulled her shoulders back, her head up, clutched her books closer to her chest. "Thanks, Mrs. Blakesly," she said, her voice catching.

Looking past Colleen, Mom gave Betsy a smile that seemed to say, "You did the right thing." A warm feeling flooded through Betsy for the first time in days.

As always, Mary Beth and Em were waiting at the corner of Main and Walnut Streets for Betsy. Before they could open their mouths, Betsy said, "Colleen's joining us this morning."

"Come on then," Mary Beth said, "don't want to be late. I'm on savings stamp duty this morning."

They were surprised to see Blackie waiting just outside the school door. He waved and Colleen's face brightened. His forehead furrowed in a frown, he hurried to Colleen, took her books under one arm, and tucked her hand inside the other elbow. Betsy, Mary Beth, and Em looked at each other and not knowing what to say, shrugged their shoulders, and went inside.

CHAPTER 23

We Will Fight Our Country's Battles

Well, Betsy thought as she pedaled onto Main Street, the words of the Marine Hymn marching through her head, maybe not the whole country's battles, but a few of the ones right here. And for her the biggest battles were fighting it out inside herself – she could hardly bear not to thank the prisoners who'd helped her, say how sorry... she could scarcely bring herself to say the words silently. In some ways having Jack know the prisoners' part of that homecoming dance nightmare was better than having to carry it alone, but still – Jack, who was always getting under her skin, why him? Why not some other fellow – someone better looking, more... a fellow who didn't get on her nerves like Jack did? And to make matters worse, here she was getting tangled up in Colleen's love life, the girl who was so stuck up she wanted nothing to do with "common girls" like Betsy.

"Betsy – wait!"

Betsy back-pedaled to a stop and turned. Rosemary and Willie hurried along the sidewalk toward her.

"We're on the way to Manweiler's," Rosemary said, a little out of breath.

Willie finished her sentence, "to find something useful for putting the posters up in shop windows and such around town. And tacks for school bulletin boards."

"Want to come along?" Rosemary offered.

Betsy checked her watch. "Sure," she said, skimming her list, "I can still finish my errands before lunch." She'd be squeezed for time, but still – she jumped at the chance to get her mind off her problems for a while and join her friends. Pushing her bike alongside so she could walk with them, she asked if they'd seen the posters yet.

Rosemary nodded, her face radiant. "I stopped in the art room during lunch hour yesterday and Leland and a couple of others were painting up a storm."

"The designs are gonna knock your socks off, Betsy." Willie told her.

Rosemary added, "Even Colleen Sherman would stop to read a poster like that."

"Speaking of . . . ," Willie gave Betsy a look.

Betsy was about to say that Colleen was too lovesick to see anything but Blackie when she heard a *"hissss-ssing"* sound. Her stomach sank. "Oh, no! Not another flat!" she said, groaning.

The three of them caught their breaths at the sight of a litter of small stones and nails, sharp ends up, trailing across the sidewalk. Willie whirled, glimpsed a shock of spiky red hair in the shadows between the brick buildings.

He marched toward that space, yanked the redhead by the elbow. "Spud Sherman, get out here." A couple of other kids trailed out, heads hanging.

"Out pulling your nasty tricks again, are you?" he scolded, with a nod toward Betsy. "Picking on a girl, you cowards. You did the damage, now fix it."

"Try and make us." Spud spit the words out. The other boys stood with hands plunged in their jacket pockets. "Besides," Spud said, glaring at Betsy who glared back, then turned away, "I'm glad she's the one that ran over it. Teach her to mind her own bees wax."

"Willie," Betsy said, forcing her voice to steady, "let them go."

Spud glared at Willie. "You deserve it, too. Chicken brother of yours." He stuck out his tongue and ran off with his gang, wrestling and elbowing each other along the way. And hooting.

"Those kids need spanking! With a razor strop. Their idea of mischief is just plain mean." Rosemary shook her head. "Gee, Betsy, both your tires and inner tubes are nothing but patches already."

"Well, I can't get new ones. Before the war's over, I'll be riding on the rims."

"Ouch!" Willie said with a grimace, then predicted, "If those brats are this mean now, they'll be jailbirds by the time they're our age."

Betsy put the kickstand down on her bike, frowned at the litter on the sidewalk. "We need to clean this up before someone else gets hurt."

"Rosemary, if you'll go in and ask Mr. Manweiler for a broom and dustpan," Willie said, "I'll stay with Betsy. I don't want her here alone. Those kids could come back."

"Oh, Willie, I'm okay," Betsy protested, "they won't do anything with people coming out to do their Saturday shopping."

"Bullies," Willie said between his teeth. "Only attack when they think no one's watching... so I'll just keep you company, okay? It only takes one person to carry a broom and dustpan a few yards."

"I'm on my way," Rosemary called and pushed through the hardware store door.

"Wish we could sweep those three up and toss them into the trash along with the mess they made," Willie muttered. He looked at Betsy, his voice softening. "Any word of your cousin Johnny yet?"

"Nothing, thanks, Willie." Betsy said, then thought to ask, "What do you hear from your brothers, if you don't mind my asking."

"The same. Neither of them can tell us much – that or they choose not to worry us by saying what's really going on. My brother on an aircraft carrier is likely in enemy waters right now, my nonviolence brother got sent from that California forest to work in an insane asylum in Minnesota. Not exactly a nonviolent place." Willie kicked at a stone.

Betsy sucked in her breath. "Seems a little like the split of beliefs in our town – but your family's is deeply personal. I'm so sorry, Willie."

Just then Rosemary came out, push broom and dustpan in hand. "Fred Hopper was the one helping me. He's as disgusted as we are and said to tell you so. Let's get this done and not waste any more time on those hoodlums."

"I'll do it," Willie said, taking the broom and sweeping with fury.

"That Sherman family...." Rosemary said, looking at Betsy. "Gee, kid, how much longer do you have to put up with Colleen sharing your room?"

Betsy shrugged, "Hard to tell," she said. Of course the whole town knew it. You couldn't keep news like that a secret, Betsy had consoled herself about her promise of secrecy to Colleen.

She sighed. "I hope not too much longer. None of her relatives in Denver will take her in, though there's some distant cousin who did offer. And her 'friends' are all snubbing her so there's no help there." She paused, then said, "Just before I left the house, Mom put Colleen in charge of Cat and Billie, and walked with Miss Grant to Mrs. Newsom's. Making a plan, I hope. And I think Blackie's married sister – *Ruth?* – is there, too. Mrs. Newsom went to collect all Colleen's belongings yesterday and is storing all but the essentials – like a few changes of clothes and toiletries, music and school books – at her house. Not room for many skirts and sweaters and shoes and coats in my closet. Gee, Rosemary, she's got more than you and I together."

Willie held the dustpan, filled to the brim now, and said, "Colleen sure turned her life upside down in a hurry."

"Can you believe it?" Rosemary let out her breath. "How could her parents disown her? Just like that? And how could she have the nerve to stand up to them?"

"I've known a couple of other kids either got kicked out by their families or left on their own for one reason or another. A few years back my brother told me about a fellow in his class who'd left home his senior year and Elmer the janitor kept a window in the gym unlocked at night so he could sleep there. No one else seemed to know about it, and the kid – a good student and swell athlete – showed up for classes every day, played football and basketball, and worked the graveyard shift at the sugar factory during the beet processing period from October through March."

They looked at one another in amazement.

"Maybe boys can be on their own better than a girl could," Betsy said, thinking that somehow Willie's family was sticking together, despite everyone else shunning Wally as a coward and a traitor.

"Do you think she'll live with Blackie's sister? I mean she isn't exactly in the right social class," Rosemary wondered. "It's a small house, but her husband's overseas, so maybe…." She shook her head, shivered, and pulled her coat closer. "Golly, you don't suppose Colleen and Blackie would do something crazy like running off together?"

Willie frowned. "What would happen to them then? Someone would go after them. I mean Blackie's about to get drafted."

"I just hope they can work something out. Soon," Betsy said and checked her watch. "Guess I'd better not go with you after all," she said. "It's going to take me longer pushing my bike than pedaling. Thanks for asking me, though...and, hey! I can't wait to see those posters around town!"

"See you later, then," Rosemary and Willie chorused.

Betsy's first stop was the post office. She'd promised Helen Martin to collect her mail as soon as it came in. She was hoping to get some letters herself – her grandparents, a pen pal, friends from the town they'd moved from – and of course all the Blakeslys were eager for news from relatives in the service.

The usual cluster of folks stood talking as they waited for Mr. Mason to distribute the bag of morning mail. Betsy had propped her bike against the building next to where the Taylors' dog, Shag, had stretched out to wait for Pete. Shag wouldn't let Spud near her bike, she was sure, and now she picked her way past Mr. Slipher, Mr. Van Brandt, Mr. Roy – all looking serious.

"The Shermans did the right thing," Mr. Slipher was saying, Mr. Van Brandt nodding in agreement. "Young people these days just don't have respect for their elders. That girl needs a good lesson and I hope her parents don't back down."

Betsy's temper boiled. She needed to get out of hearing range before she said something she'd regret. She was in no mood to hear Mr. Slipher call her "girlie" again.

"Now, Harvey," Mr. Roy was saying, "don't be too harsh. As a journalist I've learned to look at all sides of an issue, you know. For one thing, this is the 1940s, not the 1900s. And after all, she's still a child."

Pete Taylor stepped in. "He's right you know, Harvey," he said. "At the Sherman girl's age, maybe her parents need to give her a little longer leash. They're maybe a little too strict. Let her learn her lessons by experience, not strict rules, and definitely not by disowning her."

"Soft as usual, aren't you, Pete?" Mr. Slipher's jaw tightened.

"Well, you can bet she's getting her real life lesson right now. She'll come crawling back to them on her knees."

Betsy hurried along the wall opposite the rows of boxes. The minute she'd collected the mail from both Helen's and her family's boxes, she lost no time leaving.

Colleen was waiting in the kitchen when Betsy got home. And so was Mom. Billie sat on his stool having graham crackers and milk. Cat was out in the chicken house clucking at her hens.

Mom waved Colleen and Betsy to sit. Then she began to talk. "Colleen, we've found a place for you to stay."

Color draining from her cheeks, Colleen seemed to brace herself and looked up expectantly.

Mom hesitated a moment. "Unless, of course, you've changed your mind and choose to go back to your parents."

Colleen made fists of her hands, looked straight into Mom's eyes. "I haven't changed my mind. And I never will."

"Well, then, if you're truly sure, I can tell you that your friend Blackie's sister Ruth says she'll make room for you. She's coming here for dinner after church tomorrow, and we'll work out the arrangements."

"Thank you, Mrs. Blakesly," Colleen sighed. "And if you don't mind, I'd rather stay here than go to church with you. Please tell me what I can do to help get dinner ready while you're gone."

Of course Colleen wouldn't want to bump into her parents at church. At least not today, if ever, but the choir sure would miss her voice – she was the only soprano who could hit the high notes. And this was probably the end of her voice lessons in Greeley, too. People had wondered where her parents had gotten the gas to take her there every week with gas rationing and all, but they had.

But when Colleen offered to get dinner ready while the rest of them were in church, Betsy could hardly keep her jaw from dropping. This sure wasn't the Colleen she saw at school. And the way she'd stuck to her resolve made her sound at least five years older than she had a week ago.

Who's the real Colleen? Betsy wondered.

For now, though, her personal battle to have her room to herself seemed to have been fought – mostly, she had to admit, by Mom, Miss Grant, and Mrs. Newsom. Still, with luck on her side, it was one battle won.

CHAPTER 24

Beyond the Call of Duty

Betsy and Jack sat at Mrs. Newsom's kitchen table, Betsy cupping her hands around a mug of hot cider, Jack wolfing down the biggest cinnamon roll. He eyeballed the unfinished one on Betsy's plate. She pretended not to notice.

Mrs. Newsom bustled around wrapping a pan of rolls in a fresh tea towel, then adding yesterday's Denver *Post* in an attempt to keep the rolls warm. On the table a plain white card with the words *"Get well soon"* printed in large letters waited. Each of them had signed their names – *"Betsy, Jack, Mrs. Newsom."* Surely the guards would allow the card to go in with the rolls, wouldn't they?

Mrs. Newsom stopped bustling, pulled out a chair and turned to Betsy. "How's our friend Colleen doing?"

Betsy lingered over the last bite of roll, the comfort of fresh-baked bread slowing the "flight of the bumblebees" in her stomach. Nerves. Afraid to go through with this errand, afraid not to.

"It's hard to know," she said. "She comes to school every morning just before the bell rings, but hardly talks to anyone except Blackie. She did tell me during band practice one day that she's trying to adjust. One difference at a time."

Jack whistled. *"Different* – like night is from day, if you ask me. Like from living like a princess and suddenly at the last stroke of midnight the royal coach turns into a pumpkin."

"What's hard for me to understand," Betsy said, "is that Blackie's the only one who's standing by her. Her former friends treat her like she's got some awful contagious disease. And her Denver relatives have practically all turned their backs on her."

Mrs. Newsom paused, then said, "I'm sure each of them has their reasons. As for Colleen, she'll need time – lots of time – to get herself on a new path, and it's generous of Blackie's sister to take her into her home. She surely doesn't make much money working at the bank, her husband doesn't make much as a private, and now she has an extra mouth to feed."

Would Colleen look for an after-school job? Would she go to the church Ruth and Blackie's family did? The one where German was the only language spoken? Anything German drew suspicion and distrust from people like the Shermans and Sliphers. Maybe Colleen wasn't going to any church now. Betsy hadn't seen Colleen at the Methodist Church since the day her parents disowned her, and the choir didn't sound the same without her high soprano voice that could hit all the highest notes without screeching. Did Colleen miss her own church and choir? At least she was still singing in the school choir and ignoring the snubs from her 'friends.'

Jack snapped his fingers. "Say, Mrs. Newsom," he said, "didn't Ruth's father forbid her to marry Dave? A fellow from *this* side of the tracks?"

Mrs. Newsom nodded. "And Dave's parents advised him against it, too. But now the younger generation is parting ways from the old code forbidding marriage to someone 'not like us,' if you want to put it that way. And that's set off another set of problems between the generations."

Betsy leaned in, elbows propped against the red and white checked tablecloth, listening to every word. She hadn't lived in Plainsview long enough to understand why people like Mr. Slipher treated people from Mill Town as if they were – well, beneath everyone else.

Mrs. Newsom, never one to judge others, commented, "Living with Ruth gives Colleen an opportunity to experience something of what it means to marry a person from a different background. In some strange way, this may be the best thing that could have happened to her."

Betsy could see Mrs. Newsom's point, kind of, but still – how could having your own parents disown you possibly be a good thing?

Jack's brow furrowed. "She's got a rough road to travel. No more having things served to her with a silver spoon."

Mrs. Newsom stood up, wiped her hands on her apron. "Rough indeed," she agreed. She looked out the window above the kitchen sink. "And the two of you could have a rough road to the prison camp. Those are heavy storm clouds gathering. So bundle up and scoot!"

They set their plates and mugs on the counter, pulled on their jackets, and headed out to the car.

"Well," Jack said, opening the passenger door and easing Betsy in, "I sure think it's swell that Mrs. Newsom doesn't recite a long list of driving lessons when I leave like my mom does – *be careful, don't drive too fast, slow down for curves, remember to roll down your window and signal before you turn, look both ways at intersections, and on and on* – " He put the rolls carefully on Betsy's lap, saw that she was shivering.

"Gee, Betsy, what's wrong? Here, I'll grab a blanket."

The minute she'd gotten inside the car, the shivering came over her. Even her teeth were chattering.

Jack grabbed the red and black checkered lap robe from the back seat and wrapped it around her legs.

"Oh, Jack, I'm scared," she managed to say. The shivering attack had caught her by surprise. After all, taking rolls to the camp was what she'd hoped for, and now they were actually on their way. . . and she'd turned into a bundle of nerves. . . why?

She felt his hand on her arm. "It's gonna be okay, Miss Betsy B," he said, "I promise."

He shut her door, ran around to the driver's seat, got the car going, turned on the heater. The heater wasn't anything to brag about, but it began to take some of the chill from the car.

Betsy pulled the blanket close, grateful for its warmth, forced herself to take three deep breaths. Gradually her teeth stopped chattering, the shivers calmed. What a fool she'd made of herself.

She forced a smile. "I'm sorry, Jack. I'm okay now. And I suppose it'll be okay. . . but still. . . ."

"One good thing we know is that Doc Wendling requested that Sergeant Hoff be the guard who meets us."

"I'd hate to think it would be anyone but Bill," Betsy said and leaned back, leaving the driving to Jack.

Next thing she knew they were traveling south on the Greeley road. When had they left the city limits? She didn't remember passing the sugar factory, knew the column of white smoke would be bending across the road instead of rising because of the heavy clouds, had no memory of seeing the yards and yards of dirt-clogged beets waiting to be hauled inside. She hadn't heard the sounds of machines and must have ignored even the distinctive smells that visitors held their noses to avoid but to her always meant "Dad."

She checked the speedometer – 45 mph, and the bumblebees in her stomach darted nervously. The closer they got to the camp, the harder she hoped they'd learn the name of the prisoner in the hospital. If wishing made it so, Betsy told herself, there's no doubt it would come true.

As they rounded that scenic curve leading up the hill toward the camp, Betsy squinted *(She only wore her glasses at school to see the blackboard.)* toward that old barn.

"Jack, look, isn't that Mr. Slipher's car parked behind that grove of trees?"

Jack's eyesight was 20/20. He nodded, looked puzzled. "What's he so interested in here, I wonder," he said. "And I think that's the same car with the Denver license plates we saw before. You can bet he's got something up his sleeve, something for his own gain, I'd guess."

But now the car was climbing the hill, then Jack was turning onto the little gravel road leading to the camp gates. Those snarling guard dogs with their sharp fangs and eyes of steel, were racing up and down along the inside of the fence. Betsy shrank back. They were killer dogs. She pictured them attacking Helmut and Gottfried and shuddered.

Bill was waiting at the gate, reached out to shake first Betsy's, then Jack's hands. Jack handed him the still warm package. *"Ummmm, nothing like homemade rolls from Mrs. Newsom!"* Bill said, a grin spreading across his face. "Better medicine than any pills Doc Wendling could prescribe."

"How is the patient?" Jack asked the question Betsy was dying to ask.

Bill bit his lip. "He's hurt. Hurt bad. Maybe the biggest hurt is losing his buddy, but Doc says it'll be weeks before Helmut can really get around again."

Betsy winced. Helmut. She could put a face and a name together, remembering again how brave and kind he was. She said a silent Thank You.

"Well, we sure feel bad about what happened," Jack said. "I know some folks in town want to line up the whole camp in front of a firing squad, so we want this card to let him know not everybody is like that."

"So awfully good of you. A horrible tragedy. Ironic that one was killed and the other injured yet – just like the one who got hurt with the beet knife – they'll never get any badges for bravery or for having been killed or wounded in the line of duty. Who decides that, anyway?" Bill shook his head. "They're both nice young men, can't be older that either of you. They meant no harm. Just got a bad case of cabin fever, I think. And they were trying to get back in!"

A lump rose in Betsy's throat. She couldn't say a word. She trusted Bill to know something of these enemy soldiers. He spoke their language, understood them, could communicate.

Jack pulled a clean handkerchief from his pocket. Oh, golly, Betsy thought, this is the second time in the past few weeks Jack's handed her his handkerchief. Bill's eyes softened. "Not all the battles of war are fought on the so-called 'Front,' Betsy," he said. "And who's to say which ones hurt most? Which leave the deepest scars?"

He walked with them to the car, opened the door for Betsy, squared his shoulders and grinned. "Now get on home before that storm hits – and go to the movie tonight. I hear it's one with lots of songs and laughs. You Good Samaritans need a couple of hours of relief. Maybe they'll show a lighthearted movie at the camp tonight. They doctor up the newsreel parts here, though, so I won't learn much about which side's winning the current battles. Something called 'censorship,' I think."

Jack shifted into reverse and they waved good-bye. Betsy sighed. "Oh, Jack, you sure were right about this turning out to be a good thing. Those two fellows, even though they're the 'enemy' went way beyond the call of duty for me."

Snowflakes began to fly against the windshield. Jack switched on the headlights and wipers and drove carefully back toward town. At the foot of the hill, they were immediately bathed in a fiery glow. Much bigger than any homecoming parade bonfire, the old barn was going down in flames, crumbling, collapsing, crashing – sparks and ashes flying in every direction.

CHAPTER 25

Any Bonds Today?

"Can we stop and see Colleen? Please? Pretty please?" Billie tapped an impatient rhythm on the sidewalk, his child size 5 Dr. Edwards oxfords punctuating the beat.

Betsy looked down at him. "It's *'may'* not *'can.'* Remember we talked about that? When you want to ask permission, use *'may.'* We already know you can or are able to go into Pete's Drugs."

Billie stuck out his lower lip. "You know what I mean, so can we?"

When she didn't answer, he let go of the pout, and tried again. "I mean *may* we?"

She squeezed his hand and smiled. "Sure, Billie. We'll stop in after you get your haircut. Maybe we'll even order small root beer floats and sit on a stool at the counter so you can watch Colleen mix them."

Funny, Betsy thought, how Billie had almost adopted Colleen – and she him. Maybe it was because Colleen's brother was such a meanie.

The weather had turned warm after last week's snowstorm, and it felt good to have finished working. Early this morning Betsy and her friends had helped package bundles of scrap paper, and Cat and her classmates were doing the same with old nylon lingerie and cans of bacon grease. The men from Lion's Club had charge of flattened tin cans and also scrap metal, though people had long ago dug up every last bit of heavy metal lying around in the city dump, old car parts lots, rusted machinery on nearby farms, along river banks, and of course jackknives, scissors, shears, and carving knives from people's homes and garages. Maybe this time, though, someone had gone out to comb through what was left of the old barn. That fire had to be good for something besides getting rid of an eyesore, people said, shaking their heads.

Taking Billie's hand, Betsy stopped in front of the giant chart outside the city hall, pointed out how high the figures had climbed – and how much farther to go toward the next goal for each drive. Savings bonds topped the list. That's why the radio kept playing the song *"Any bonds today?"* to remind people that "bonds buy bombs."

The instant Billie spotted the red-and-white striped barber's pole, he let go of Betsy's hand and skipped ahead. Once inside the door, he called to Joey Sullivan, who was brandishing his polishing cloth back and forth over Mr. Van Brandt's black dress shoe. "Guess what, Joey?"

Joey looked up. Mr. Van Brandt frowned, pulled out his pocket watch.

Betsy took Billie's hand again. "Please apologize, Billie. You've interrupted Joey's work and Mr. Van Brandt is in a hurry."

Billie's cheeks flushed. "I'm sorry I was rude, Sir."

Joey gave him a wink and a grin, eased Mr. Van Brandt's foot to the floor and stood. The banker pulled out a quarter and pressed it into Joey's palm.

"Thanks very much, Sir," Joey said and put the coin in his small money pouch. Did Joey get to keep the money he earned, Betsy wondered, or did he give it to his father? She knew they had a large family – an even dozen – and lived in a two-story frame house on the edge of town. "Catholics," folks whispered. "Irish." Betsy wasn't sure why people whispered the word "Catholics." What was wrong with that? As for Joey, he had a ready smile, a twinkle in his big blue eyes, a cheery word for everyone. And he whistled like a songbird.

"Have a seat," the barber greeted them. "You're third in line, Master Blakesly."

"Thanks, Mr. Willowby," Billie said. "How old do I have to be before you call me 'Mr.' instead of 'Master'?"

The other men in the shop chuckled. "Got you on that one, didn't he, Clyde?" Hank Schiff kidded. Billie squirmed.

Mr. Willowby paused, scissors and comb suspended above Mr. Slipher's head. "Maybe about the time you need a shave along with your haircut I might promote you, Master Blakesly. Till then I promise to give your chair a couple of spins after each cut."

Billie grinned from ear to ear. "Gee, thanks, Mr. Willowby."

"Are you going to be a chemist like your dad, Billie?" a man named Mr. Schiller asked.

Why do grownups always ask little kids that question? Betsy wondered.

That didn't seem to bother her brother, though. He held up the black leather aviator cap on his lap, the one he wore summer, winter, and everything in between. To bed if Mom would let him. "No," he said. "I'm going to be a B-26 pilot and win the war."

"Good for you, young feller," Mr. Schiller said and made the victory sign.

The men began to talk among themselves – "... something suspicious about that fire...." Sam Ruhl was saying.

Wayne Weber from the Conoco station chimed in, "– whole place reeks of burned rubber and gasoline. I oughta know – I smell those smells every day of the week."

Betsy watched Billie's eyes widen. She could almost see the wheels inside his head storing this information and wondering what it meant. She'd heard rumors of all kinds. Was this a case of arson? Or an accident – like a cigarette tossed carelessly away? Arson or accident, who would have been in that abandoned barn? And why? They'd talked about it at home. All the kids at school talked about it between classes, walking to and from school. Whispers even passed from one person to the next during choir practice.

"Too bad the town's one and only cop can't do much more than hand out traffic tickets," Editor Roy Ray said. "Heck, there's so little car and truck traffic these days the only traffic ticket he hands out is to some kid who forgets to arm signal a turn or a stop on his bike."

"Time to hire a detective – how about Dick Tracy?" Mr. Van Brandt called, drawing a chorus of laughter.

In the brief silence after the door closed, Betsy became aware of a current of background sounds – shoes scuffling against the black and white checked linoleum, someone coughing, another blowing his nose. Clyde began untying the barber apron protecting Mr. Slipher's pin-striped suit, brushing the hairs from his neck.

Mr. Slipher adjusted his bow tie, addressed the room in general. "I knew something bad would happen. We should have drilled holes in all those Heinies. Bunch of jailbirds."

Editor Ray looked at him. "So you're accusing them of setting that old barn on fire? And who else might be guilty? Someone who lives in Mill Town? They're German, too. What about the rest of us? After all, America is the great melting pot of the world. Who even knows whether he's got a drop or two of German in his blood mix?"

"Not a drop in my blood, I'm proud to say," Mr. Slipher announced.

Clyde turned his customer's head toward the poster on the wall, then the one in the window. "Now Harvey, get off that high horse – nobody's accused anybody of starting that fire or committing other crimes. We're trying for a little civility here. See those posters? That one – *'Hate breeds hate'* and in the window – *'We are all members of the human race'*... and I, for one, won't stand for any hate talk in my shop. Nothing personal, understand. But think it over."

Betsy swelled with pride. Leland's bright posters with their clean designs caught everyone's eye and a band of eager sophomores had succeeded in placing them in every store window and school, the Carnegie library and post office. Even Mr. Slipher gave in and let them post one in a dark corner of the theatre lobby. Clyde was using those posters exactly the way they were intended. Not that Mr. Slipher would change his ways, but maybe if he heard it said enough, he'd at least tone it down.

When Billie's hair was cut, the barber let him choose which penny sucker he wanted – red, green, yellow, or purple. "Yellow, please," Billie said. "For lemonade in summer."

As they left, Betsy suggested he put the sucker in his pocket for later since they'd be stopping for root beer floats. Mom and Dad were pretty strict about how much candy they could have. Maybe it helped that candy was one of the biggest war shortages.

The bell on the drugstore's door announced their arrival. Saturday shoppers browsed the aisles or sat in booths chatting and laughing over glasses of cherry or chocolate Cokes. Billie spotted Colleen right away, called, and waved. Betsy helped him up onto a red-cushioned stool at the counter in front of the row of spigots for root beer, Coke, water, and lemonade Colleen was operating. Farther down the counter two men – one dipping his spoon into a banana split, the other a double chocolate sundae with chocolate syrup, nuts, and a maraschino cherry – seemed to be having a serious discussion of some sort. They didn't look up.

Pete Taylor leaned from the prescriptions lab window. "Keep a close eye on my new soda fountain girl for me, will you Billie? We don't want her to skimp on your serving – or get the wrong order."

On the other side of the counter Colleen, wearing the Pete's Drugs apron and only a touch of lipstick, looked, Betsy thought... well, not at all like the school glamour queen. Except for her crowning glory – thick auburn hair. "Hi there, Billikins, this must be a special treat. I see you've just come from the barbershop."

Hmmm – *"Billikins."* Betsy winced. He put up a fuss if she or Cat called him that. Made him sound like a baby, he claimed.

"Two special treats," Billie said, beaming. "The first is I get to see you, the second is a small root beer float. One for me, one for Betsy."

Colleen reached for a pair of glasses the right size and shape. "Coming right up," she said, brightening, "I think this is an order I can fill without any mistakes."

The bell on the door rang again. Billie looked up and waved. "Hi, Fred. We're having root beer floats!"

"Ummm, wish I could have one, too, or maybe a strawberry ice cream cone, but I'm on an errand for Mr. Manweiller and have to hurry right back." He looked across the counter. "Pete's got himself a mighty pretty girl to mix up those ice cream treats!"

That brought a smile to Colleen's face. "Looks aren't everything, Fred, but thanks. As for being a soda jerk, I probably qualify to get on *"Major Bowes Amateur Hour."*

Betsy could never have imagined Colleen acting like a real person, the way she was now, but still – she couldn't help feeling sorry for herself. First Billie, now Fred – acting as if she weren't even present. At school she hadn't cared a pin about Colleen and her snobbish friends. But this was different. After all, she was the one who'd rescued Colleen and now – Colleen was the star of the show. If Colleen's world had turned upside down, Betsy's world sure wasn't the same as it used to be, either.

Fred collected a prescription from Pete, then tapped Betsy's shoulder on his way to the door. "And how's my favorite dance partner these days?" he asked, then looked over at the poster in the window, "I hear we can thank those sassy sophomores for the swell posters."

Betsy felt her face flush. Oh, golly, she thought, there I go blushing again. Would she ever get over it? She looked at the poster, too, and said, "Leland designed them. He's really good. And a couple of other art students helped do the painting."

"Another team effort," Fred said, and winked. "Good work!"

He headed out the door, called back, "Thanks, Pete," turned to wave at Colleen, Billie, and Betsy. "See you around!"

"Ummm, this sure is swell." Billie sipped root beer from his straw, feeling very grown up since he'd finally mastered that trick, took the long-handled spoon and brought up a generous bite of vanilla ice cream.

"So do I pass the root beer float-making test?" Colleen asked.

Billie made the victory sign with his left hand.

"Best one I've ever had," Betsy said, holding each bite on her tongue till it melted. "Gee, Colleen, I sure hope you're doing okay. It has to be hard. Do you wish maybe you'd gone to live in Denver with the friends of your aunt and uncle?"

Colleen's jaw tightened. "If I'd gone away, you know what people would say." Her lips trembled a moment, then said in a low voice, "They'd say Blackie got me in trouble and I had to leave town till after. . . you know. I'm staying here to prove that's not true. They'll have to find something else to gossip about."

Billie stopped spooning ice cream. "Trouble? What kind of trouble?"

Colleen said, "No trouble, Billie. Just something some people want to make up. So put that right out of your head, okay? Besides, Blackie comes over after supper every evening and we do our home-work at Ruth's kitchen table. Ruth and I sure were glad he was there when we that air raid siren went off last night. Made us feel safer, I guess. So everything's fine."

He grinned, nodded, and slurped up the last of the root beer.

Jack was just leaving the bakery when they stepped out of the drugstore. "Hi, Betsy! Hold the phone a minute, okay?"

"What does that mean, Betsy," Billie wanted to know. "You're not talking on the phone."

"He just means to wait a minute. He probably wants to tell us something.

"I wish big people would just say what they mean," Billie said. "I'm not going to be like that when I get big."

"Good for you, Billie, but I hope Jack keeps it short. We need to get home."

In a couple of giant steps, Jack was there, made sure to put himself on the street side. He did know his manners, Betsy reminded herself. He treated her like a lady, just the way Dad treated Mom. And Betsy and Cat and other ladies and girls, too.

"Hi, there, Bill." Jack gave the youngster a big wink. "You're looking neat as a pin with that brand new crew cut... ready to fly that plane!"

Billie grinned. Jack had called him "Bill" like he was an equal.

"We both need to get home, Betsy, so we'll just keep walking to your house, but I have a couple of things to tell you." He slowed his pace to match Betsy and Billie's, but knew he was impatient to move faster.

"So what's this I need to know about?" She gave him a look that said, 'Is this something to talk about with Mr. Big Ears here?'

Jack read her look. After all, he had two younger sisters, so he knew what she meant. "Well, first – and I can't say much about this yet, but – the volunteer firemen? The ones who put out that fire before it got out of control?" He paused. "Seems maybe that barn was being used for storing stuff to sell on the black market. There's a lot of money in that."

Billie said nothing. Betsy hoped he didn't know what the "black market" was. But a light bulb turned on when he said that. It all added up, what she and Jack had noticed twice now at that place. "Interesting," she said. "So do you think anything will be done about that?"

Jack shrugged. "Probably not. At least not anything they'd print in the *Sun* next week along with all the war news and letters from local guys in the service."

They didn't need to say more. If Mr. Slipher had been dealing in the black market with somebody from Denver, then things would probably be kept quiet. Right or wrong. Because it was "respected citizens" who'd be named on both sides. Dealer and buyers.

Betsy didn't dare say a word with Billie here, but she sure planned to talk with Mom and Dad after Cat and Billie were in bed tonight.

Jack stopped and turned to her. "And here's the second thing. You don't have to give me an answer right now, but think it over and talk to your parents before you decide." The words practically exploded out.

What in the world was he going to ask her?

"My parents," he said, seeming to think how best to explain this, "have been wanting to see this program in Greeley at their concert hall. It's coming up next week and they've saved their gas rationing stamps and ticket money for our family plus one extra ticket since there's room in the car, and – well, we wondered if you'd be our guest."

Her breath caught. That sure came out of nowhere. True, his mother was a talented pianist, his next younger sister played cello, and Jack, of course, played French horn. Probably seeing that program was his mother's idea. But why would they ask her along?

She tried to put her thoughts together. She'd never gone to anything like that in Greeley, though Dad and Mom had taken her along a few times to the Denver Auditorium for a stage play or concert. And twice in winter they'd all gone to see the Ice Follies.

Stalling for time, she asked, "A program? In Greeley? What kind of program?"

"Oh, gosh, Betsy, I would leave out the most important thing. It's a whole troop of Cossacks from Russia. They perform special native Russian dances wearing their original native dress. Pretty athletic dances, Mom says, not that I know."

"That's very nice of your parents, Jack," she said. "I'll talk it over with Mom and Dad this evening."

"It sure would be swell if you'd go with us, Betsy. We all want you."

They were at the Blakeslys' door now and Billie hadn't said a word, just taking everything in, it seemed. So what would he come up with once she brought up the subject at supper tonight? Before that, though, she'd phone Mary Beth. Mary Beth was easy to talk to and she'd keep it to herself. Would accepting Jack's invitation get her "labeled" at school as his girlfriend? She didn't want that.

"So, tomorrow then?" she said. But then – going to Greeley – at night – for a concert – and, after all, Jack had been a good friend. If Colleen could say, *"Who cares what people think?"*, why couldn't she? Still, she needed time before giving Jack an answer.

"Right," he said and sprinted off.

~ ~ ~

Author's Note

World War II defined my teenage years. The Japanese attack on Pearl Harbor December 7, 1941 happened a few months after my twelfth birthday. The Allies won victory over the Axis nations in 1945 – first in April over Italy and Germany (European Front), then in September over Japan (Pacific Front) two months after I turned sixteen.

Because of my father's profession, during those four years our family lived in three different Great Western Sugar Company towns in northeastern Colorado. We were in Johnstown when the war began and the following summer the company promoted Dad to a position at the Windsor factory where we stayed three years. The summer of 1945 another move took us to Fort Morgan. Six weeks later, the war ended. Through those moves from town to town, Denver – where both sets of my grandparents lived – remained our "home base." Gas rationing, along with that of oil and rubber, forced us to limit how often we could travel to Denver. Throughout the war years everyone was willing to "do without" so that the troops could be properly armed and fed. The air we breathed bristled with Patriotism – with a capital "P."

War Bonds is based on my memories of those years, particularly the ones in Windsor (which I've called Plainsview in the book) when the prisoner of war camp was built several miles east and south of Windsor on the road to Greeley. While the story is based on my memories of those years, the characters and the story line are fiction.

What I hope the reader may gain from the story is a taste of what life was like in the 1940s and something about the impact the war made on a way of life we'd taken for granted. Because what I have written is limited by the point of view of an impressionable teenage girl, I've added a list of resources for those who choose to explore this place and time in our nation's history.

And a few after words –

Stories have a way of connecting past to present that enlarges and enlightens memories. And so it has been for me – at class reunions decades after the war years; when particular topics arise in casual conversations with friends and strangers; in books and films and museums – past and present weave increasingly more threads into the fabric of my teen years.

Class reunions gather people together who shared the same moment in history and who now see that moment in time from a more informed perspective.

During my 50-year Windsor class reunion, my friend Jody and I were reminiscing about our World War II experiences at harvest time picking potatoes in Mr. Fritzler's field and recounting memories about the German prisoners of war. Jody's marriage had taken her to Scottsdale, Arizona during those intervening years and she'd recently gone for a dental appointment there. Making conversation, the dentist asked her where she'd grown up. When she answered "Colorado," he wanted to know which town. "Oh, just a little town," she said, "too small to be on most maps, but it's about 50 miles north of Denver – and a nice drive up the Big Thompson River in the Rocky Mountains." Still he pressed her for the town's name. When she answered, "Windsor," his face widened into a smile. "I do know Windsor," he said, adding something like this, "You see, I was a prisoner of war in that camp outside of town. When the war was over and we'd all been sent back to Germany, I knew I wanted to become a citizen of the United States."

It wasn't until our 60th reunion that a pair of classmates who'd enrolled in our junior year could bring themselves to tell us (voices soft, words brief) that they had been among those Japanese-Americans who lived in the internment (also called "relocation") camp Amache on arid land in southeastern Colorado.

Each alluded to what life was like then when they were treated as enemies – prisoners stripped of their land and possessions. What they weren't reluctant to talk about was their enormous gratitude toward Governor John Carr – first, for being one of the few governors to welcome these "spies" and, at the camp's closing, for seeing to it that they had a place to start their lives.

While each story I connected to personally touched my heart, perhaps the one most poignant is this:

Some 20 years or more after the war my husband and I were educators in Fort Morgan, Colorado – my husband as an elementary school principal and I as a high school English teacher. One fall the district welcomed an exchange scholar from Germany who would teach German at the high school. He was assigned to the classroom next door to mine. His wife and young son came, too, and the boy enrolled in my husband's school.

Several times we invited the visiting family to share supper with us. One evening Hans and my husband began to talk of their experiences during World War II. Hans had been trained from an early age as a Hitler Youth, subsequently seeing action during the thick of the war. The two men discovered they'd been on the same battlefield at one point in the war. A hush fell over the room – our children's eyes opened wide. I don't know what the children were thinking, but we four grownups couldn't help but imagine that the two fathers at our table now may have been aiming guns and grenades at one another. That story's ending for Hans was that he'd been among those taken prisoner and shipped to an American prison camp in a southern state.

After a moment he looked up. "If I hadn't been a prisoner," he said in a quiet solemn voice, "I'd never have understood what freedom is."

Sources

A Walk Through Windsor: 1940-1980, Mary Alice Lindblad

The *Windsor Beacon* issues from 1941-1945 - Windsor-Severance Public Library

Greeley History Museum - 714 8th Street, Greeley, CO

Fort Morgan History Museum - 404 Main Street, Fort Morgan, CO

World War II Resources, National Archives, Washington, D. C.

World War II German Prisoners of War in Larimer & Weld Counties,
     Pioneer Association, Fort Collins, CO, 2011

A VERY SHORT LIST OF SUGGESTIONS FOR SOURCES TO EXPLORE:

Life on the Home Front

Dancing in Combat Boots, Teresa B. Funke, 2009

– a collection of real life stories about women finding ways to help with the war effort

The All-Girl Filling Station's Last Reunion, Fannie Flagg, 2013

– a novel recalling the tactics a family of sisters used to keep their father and brothers'
gas station in business during the war years, both hilarious and poignant in tone,
revealing of daily life at the time

Germans from Russia in northern Colorado

Second Hoeing, Hope Williams Sykes, University of Nebraska Press, 1982

– a fictional account of the problems encountered by a first generation teenage girl set
in a rural community north of Fort Collins

From the Steppes to the Prairie (nonfiction), Eloise Sagel Hanson, 1984
    Centennial Commission of the City of Fort Morgan

The Sugar Beet Industry

Footprints in Sugar: A History of Great Western Sugar Company, Candy Hamilton, 2009

Sugar Tramp: Colorado's Great Western Railway, Gary Morgan, 1975

History Museums in Loveland, Fort Morgan, Greeley, and others

Japanese Relocation or Internment Camps during World War II

Nissei: The Quiet Americans, Bill Hosokawa, 1969

– a personal account of the author's experiences in a "relocation" camp in Wyoming.
Hosokawa was 27 years old when he, along with his wife and young child were ordered
to the camp. The book encompasses a larger view of his life to that point as well as of
the impact of being "prisoners in their own land" made on them.

Tall Grass, Sandra Dallas, 2007

– a fiction story of life at Amache relocation camp in southwestern Colorado

Colorado History Museum, Denver, CO, exhibition of a family's living quarters
    at Camp Amache

Some topics to explore about Betsy's fictional story and about the 1940s

– The book's title, *War Bonds*, refers literally to sales of treasury bonds that financially supported the costs of war. In what ways was money spent to ensure that the Allies could defeat the Axis nations?

The term "war bonds" suggests links or connections between individuals or groups. A "bond" may be one of friendship or one of bondage. Bonds can be created – or broken – between individuals or groups. What does the story suggest about these kinds of bonds? In what ways might war create bonds that wouldn't happen otherwise?

Following World War I attempts to form a League of Nations failed, but the notion of "linking hands" with other nations did not die. Following World War II, the United Nations was born. Research the thread of this effort and identify its leaders and what motivated them.

– Betsy becomes more aware of prejudice in the town as the story evolves. For one thing, people from Mill Town are looked down on for living "on the wrong side of the tracks."

What motivates her to try to make changes? Does Betsy herself have feelings of prejudice that she may or may not be aware of? Have you felt prejudiced against – or toward – in certain situations? What were the circumstances? Describe how that affected you.

– In what ways have prejudices against those regarded as being "different" from what society finds "acceptable" changed following the 1940s?

Research the decision to place West Coast Japanese-Americans in "relocation" or internment camps. (What does each of these terms suggest?) How does putting these citizens in camps square with President Roosevelt's words that "the only thing we have to fear is fear itself"? (U.S. citizens of both German and Italian heritage were also viewed with some element of prejudice and fear, but it was the Japanese Americans who could be easily identified and set apart.)

– If the war should go on long enough that Willie is drafted, which of his two older brothers would he choose to follow as his model: to serve in the military or declare himself a pacifist?

– What forms of propaganda does the government use to influence citizens' attitudes? Is there a connection between propaganda and censorship? In what ways might propaganda and censorship be used in either a positive or a negative way?

– What caused the various types of shortages during World War II? What are some of the inventions that resulted from having shortages?

continued on next page

Topics to explore

continued from previous page

– The sugar beet industry dominated much of northeastern Colorado and neighboring states during a major portion of the 20th century. Research this history.

This industry drew many Germans from Russia to settle here. What is their story?

– Interview someone who lived during the World War II years – starting with someone from your own family, and ask them to remember how they experienced life then.

– Investigate how the cartoonish *"Kilroy was Here"* that appeared here, there, and everywhere during those years originated.

– Besides those who served as medical workers, journalists and reporters went unarmed into fields of battle. Search for the stories behind one or more of those journalists or editorial cartoonists. In what ways might their stories compare and contrast with those serving in the current "war against terrorists"?

– Think about the widely known quotation *"My country right or wrong"* and how that principle applied to the attitudes toward patriotism during the Second World War.

– If rationing became a new way of life for you today, what things would it be hardest for you to give up or to enjoy only on rare occasions? How would that make your attitude toward life change?

The author (far right) and family - Windsor, Colorado, 1943.

Made in the USA
San Bernardino, CA
21 January 2015